you had your chance, lee burrows

piper rayne

about you had your chance, lee burrows

Lee f'ing Burrows
The Kingsmen's star quarterback.
Legendary throwing arm.
Six-pack abs.
Kissable lips.

Oh, but don't forget, he's also a lying, heartless egomaniac who broke my heart in college.

It took me years to build myself back up after his deceit, and now I have the dream opportunity to prove myself working as a sports therapist for a professional team.

The hurdle? Or mountain to be more accurate…
The job is with the San Francisco Kingsmen.

Back when I was a naïve college girl, I felt lucky that he even noticed me. Now eight years later, *he'd* be lucky if I gave *him* the time of day.

Which I won't. Not ever.

Some people don't deserve a second chance and Lee Burrows is one of them.

Now if someone could only tell him that because he's hell-bent on scoring the winning touchdown and won't accept that it's game over for us.

YOU HAD YOUR CHANCE, Lee Burrows

one

. . .

Lee

BEEP! I honk my horn and shine my brights at the car in front of me, but instead, the windshield wipers run back and forth on the windshield.

"Shit." I scour the steering wheel of my new Denali for the damn brights, but the car in front of me moves to the right-hand lane just as I figure out how to stop the wipers.

Thank god for tinted windows, because if a fan saw me being a prick on the US101 toward Santa Clara, they'd tweet, post, and share it with the world. And then I'd be cast as an asshole in the gossip blogs. But I cannot be late on the first day of training camp, especially during a contract year.

My phone rings through my Bluetooth, so I glance at the screen. Joran, my agent, surely has a checklist of players he needs to talk to this morning, since calling the first morning of training camp is a yearly ritual for him. In truth, the guy is a pain in the ass, but he gets shit done with a line of zeros on my contracts, so I can't complain.

I hit the accept button on my steering wheel. "Hey, Joran."

"How's my favorite Canadian football player?"

"I'm your *only* client from Canada who plays football." I check my blind spot over my shoulder and change lanes, pushing down on the accelerator. Coach doesn't accept tardiness, not even from his number one guy—me.

"Semantics," he says before I hear his muffled voice, his hand over the receiver, talking to his assistant.

I chuckle. At least he owns his shit lines.

There's no way Joran enjoys his life. I could see him stopping midorgasm with a panting woman under him to take a call. That's also what makes him the best in the business.

"Wanted to check in and see how you're feeling about today."

"Same as every year. Got some nerves, but nothing I can't stifle." I veer into the right lane to pass another guy who thinks he should be in the left lane.

"Attaboy. The better you do this season, the bigger the contract."

It's unlike Joran to say something so obvious. Usually, he's balls to the wall, telling you how great you are and nerves are for the weak.

He's not wrong though. My fingers tighten on the steering wheel. My contract with the San Francisco Kingsmen ends after this season, so I can't afford any injuries. If the choice is mine, I want to remain with the Kingsmen, but if they do release me, I don't want to give another team a reason to lowball me.

I love the life I've built in San Francisco. The city, my teammates, and the coaching staff are awesome. I've got a good thing going here, and I'm not ready for it to end. My childhood taught me what it feels like when a good thing ends and I'm not a fan, nor do I want to repeat it.

"Yeah, I know, Joran. Don't worry, I've worked extra hard this off-season. I'm primed and ready and focused." I'm eager to get off the phone and listen to my music that will pump me up.

"Glad to hear it. All right, well, just wanted to wish you

luck. We'll touch base later this week to see how things are developing."

"Sounds good." I hit end call, beating Joran because he never says goodbye. On to the next paycheck for him.

The sign for my exit comes up and I pull off the interstate toward the performance facility situated right next to the Kingsmen stadium.

After I park my car, gather my shit, and go inside, it doesn't take long before I'm met with the familiar faces of my teammates and coaching staff in the hallways. I say a quick hello to all of them but continue on my way, anxious to get the first day of training camp over with. My nerves always dissipate after my first throw. As long as it's a good one and lands in the hands of one of our receivers.

I walk into the locker room to my locker.

"You ready to do this?" My teammate and best friend, Miles Cavanaugh, stands in front of his locker next to me.

Miles and I played together at University of Michigan and somehow were lucky enough to end up on the same team a couple years ago.

"Ready as ever."

He pulls me in for a brief hug before I drop my bag in front of my locker. All my gear neatly hangs in its designated spots. Along with my helmet, my locker holds all the team shorts and shirts emblazoned with my number and name for upcoming days like today, when I guarantee we'll find out who sat on their ass all off-season versus those who didn't. I never tire of seeing my name on the back of an NFL jersey, and I try to never take for granted that my dream has come true.

"Fuck, Cavanaugh, it's too early in the season to smell that shit." Darius Jones, one of our defensive ends, steps into the locker room and covers his nose with his shirt. "How can you sit next to him while he drinks that, Burrows?"

"I think I've grown immune to it over the years," I say.

Miles is known for his juice cleanses and any new healthy fad. I swear every single one of them should have a warning, *may need nose plug to consume.*

"What happened to the dreads?" I ask Darius. His hair is cropped close to his rich brown skin.

"Had to make myself less appealing. Too many ladies wanted a piece of me."

The locker breaks into laughter, easing some of the tension. Some of the guys are shoo-ins for this season, but some are still chasing the dream. Unfortunately, by the end of training camp, the roughly ninety players in this locker room will be cut to fifty-three.

"I gotta take a piss. I'll catch you at the meeting," Miles says and leaves.

I chitchat with a few guys as I change into Kingsmen's athletic gear. Now things get real.

When it's time, I walk into the auditorium and sit next to Miles.

"We're going to have a good season. I can feel it," he says, rubbing his hands together.

I whip my head in his direction. "Jesus Christ, Miles. You're tempting fate!"

His forehead wrinkles. "I don't believe in that bullshit."

"Everyone knows that's the kiss of death."

He shakes his head at me. "You honestly don't think we can do this?"

I'm superstitious, while Miles is the only player I've ever met who has never reworn socks, stopped shaving, or had some routine at every game for fear of losing a winning streak. "I didn't say that. But it's not something you say like it's a sure thing."

"We have everything we need. Hell, Brady Banks at receiver and you at quarterback." He puts his hands in the air. "Dream Team." And he shrugs like the cocky asshole he isn't.

"You've got me at safety on defensive. Pick sixes all day long." He pretends to catch a ball and run.

I can't stop laughing at my best friend. He's really not conceited, so when he pretends to be, I enjoy every minute of it.

He turns to me, seeing I'm still not convinced he just put a spell on us. "Whether we say it or not doesn't change the outcome. It's our hard work, our confidence, and our attitude that will get us to the Super Bowl." He smacks my shoulder. "And that big contract you're looking for."

I shake my head, not wanting to think about my contract at this moment even if it looms above me like a dark cloud.

Thankfully, Coach Baker walks through the side door, the rest of the coaching staff following him like little baby ducks crossing a road. "What is this, kindergarten? Quiet the fuck down!"

His booming voice grabs everyone's attention and it turns dead silent.

He smiles, happy he still has the authority to get us to do anything he wants. "Welcome."

The room laughs. Coach Baker isn't a hard-ass, but he is someone to fear. He's all about hard work and dedication.

"Okay, for you newbies, I'm Coach Baker…" He continues down the line, introducing all our coaches and staff. Lastly, he signals to Dr. Carlisle, our head athletic trainer. "And when you get injured, here is the man you see."

Dr. Carlisle steps forward, shaking hands with Coach Baker as though they didn't talk to one another minutes earlier. His short light-brown hair is perfectly gelled, and he's dressed in the Kingsmen polo and khaki shorts as if he's ready for his endorsement deal. I think the guy is kind of a dick—he thinks he's a celebrity, bragging about his Instagram following—but he's kept me healthy all these years, so who am I to judge.

"Thanks." He turns to us in the stands. "I'm Doctor

Carlisle, Head Athletic Director. I look forward to having a great season with you all and doing our department's part to keep you healthy. I'll start by introducing our staff members. For you veterans, we only have one new addition this year."

The group of athletic trainers comes out and I'm busy cracking my neck from my shitty sleep last night, so I don't bother looking as he says the names I'm already familiar with.

"Oh shit," Miles whispers.

"What?" I ask, looking down right as she emerges from the group. All the air in my lungs seizes as though I've been sacked by a three-hundred-pound nose tackle.

"It's her, right?" Miles turns to me. "Shayna—"

"Kudrow," I finish for him, my eyes locked on her.

It's her, the woman I screwed over in college.

The same woman I've never stopped thinking about.

two

· · ·

Shayna

You got this, Shayna. Deep breaths. Deep breaths.

I place my hand over my stomach to calm it. I swear acrobats are inside, practicing their tumbling act.

The first day of any new job is nerve racking. The first day of a new job in a new city, even more so. But the first day working alongside the man who broke your heart brings on a whole new anxiety level. Especially when the man is the star quarterback and captain of the team.

I've spent eight years avoiding the fact Lee Burrows even exists. If his picture came on the TV, I'd change the channel. If I found myself in a sports store, I'd avoid the football section. And if I'd scroll past his picture with some beautiful woman on a social media gossip site, I'd click off the page. I definitely didn't stop and zoom in to see what kind of woman caught his eye these days. Spoiler, they were all the complete opposite of me.

Okay, my willpower waned a few times, but I quickly realized how miserable seeing him with someone else made me and how it forced me to question all the self-confidence I'd rebuilt since college. So yeah, I recently stopped, but the important thing is I'm on the road to recovery.

But it doesn't mean I don't think about him all the time.

The plus side is I no longer think of him through the haze of a girl infatuated with a boy she thinks she can never have. Now I think of him with narrowed eyes because I realize what a snake he really is.

His affable, good old boy charm is a front for a lying, manipulative, self-serving asshole.

And with that reminder, I wrap my hand around the door handle to the San Francisco Kingsmen's training facility and walk inside, ready to face him. I've been to the training facility for my interviews as well as last week to familiarize myself with the space, so I head straight down to the head physician's office to say I'm here.

I did my introductory interview with Dr. Frampton, who I really like, since Dr. Carlisle was traveling at the time the position was announced, but I did my final interview with Dr. Carlisle. He's… intimidating to be sure. He has strong feelings and isn't afraid to express them, even if it might come across as belittling or rude sometimes.

Still, he's the head of one of the best medical teams in the NFL and neither he, nor that jerk Lee Burrows, was going to prevent me from accepting my dream position. When I got a job with a professional team after loving football all my life, I could have pinched myself.

After all, a quarterback's career is relatively short lived, whereas I can spend my entire career with the Kingsmen. So putting up with Lee until he retires in a few years is an acceptable trade-off for the chance to do what I've always wanted.

Besides, Lee already screwed me over once. Like hell I'll let him do it again by turning down this job because it might be awkward between us. I'm no longer the shy, mousy girl he knew in college. I've worked hard to develop the self-confidence I always had before he entered my life.

I arrive outside Dr. Frampton's office and knock on the doorjamb since the door is open.

He glances up from the paper in his hand and takes off his reading glasses. "Good morning, Shayna. Ready for today?"

I smile and step inside. "Good morning. A little nervous, truth be told."

He nods and offers me a nice, understanding smile. "First day with the athletes. I get it. But just remember, we wouldn't have hired you if we didn't think you could handle the level of testosterone within these walls."

I chuckle. "Fair enough."

He stands from his desk. "I was just about to head down to see if Dr. Carlisle is ready to head out to the field with the players. Coach Baker always starts training camp with an info session for all the new players, part of which is introducing staff to everyone."

I nod because talking right now isn't an option. The words "players" and "introduction" are lodged in my brain. My first run-in with Lee will be standing before him where he can examine me for as long as he wants, and I'll have to ignore the fact his eyes are even on me.

Oh please, Shayna, you're probably long forgotten in his head.

He grabs a tablet off his desk and walks around it to stand in front of me. "I can see you're nervous, but don't be. These may be the guys you've been watching on TV for years, but at the end of the day, they're people just like you and me. And they need us." He winks.

"Okay." I nod again, suppressing a cringe. Dr. Frampton doesn't know my history with their top player.

Great. My reluctance at coming face-to-face with Lee again has made one of my bosses think I'm all starry-eyed at the prospect of being around professional athletes. Professional athletes that it's my job to put my hands on to make them feel better. I could strangle Lee all over again.

Don't get me wrong, I've long been a bit of a football nut and it'll be strange to be working with athletes I've cheered on from my couch for years, but that's not what has me so nervous.

With any luck, Lee won't recognize me or will have forgotten me entirely. As much as that would piss me off, it would make my life a heck of a lot easier.

I follow Dr. Frampton out of his office. We have a quick meeting with the rest of the medical team, most of whom I've already met, before heading to the big meeting room where all the players and coaching staff are.

My breakfast bubbles up in my stomach and I paste on an air of confidence. I'm more than capable of doing this job and doing it great, but there's always the question of what my new coworkers—and my bosses—will think when they see me in action. Not to mention setting eyes on Lee in person for the first time in years. He's the star of the show around here, and even if I'm probably going to want to spit in his face when I see him, I can never let anyone know.

While Dr. Carlisle waits for Coach Baker to introduce him, I stand behind him, silently repeating my mantra that I have this. Lee isn't all that. He's just a guy who wronged me. No one special.

But when Dr. Carlisle says my name, I step out from behind him, smiling and giving a small wave to the players, quickly scanning the room for one man in particular.

He's right in the middle, as anyone of his caliber would be.

My breath catches.

Lee Burrows.

The man who made me feel both the highest and lowest I ever have in my life.

Of course, I know what he looks like these days. It's hard not to be aware of what the number one quarterback in the country looks like, but the magazines and television don't do him justice.

He's as attractive as ever, but the boy has grown into a man. His brown wavy hair is cropped short on the sides, and his angular jaw is covered in a dusting of facial hair. Even covered by his shirt and shorts, there's no doubt his muscles are bigger and stronger. The fact that he's still as hot as ever is an annoying truth I'll have to deal with.

But it's his look of shock that gives me satisfaction. His mouth hangs open and he blinks his hazel eyes a few times as if he's a genie who can clear me from his vision.

Dr. Carlisle carries on, talking about how each of the players will be meeting with the medical staff to undergo an assessment over the next couple of days, but Lee's gaze doesn't stray from me. It's like a spider crawling over my skin.

Okay, maybe not a spider. Maybe more like a single finger dragging slowly over my heated skin, but big whoop. It's still annoying.

My willpower betrays me and I glance his way a couple of times. That's when I spot him looking beside him at Miles—clearly those two are still thick as thieves. Miles catches me looking and slowly nods with a wry smile.

I shift in place since they're both looking at me, and I listen intently to Coach Baker as he gives the guys a rundown of the morning's plans. He lists off a few players who need to come with the medical staff for their workups, and I'm finally able to escape Lee's intrusive gaze.

As soon as I step out of his view, I rest my back on a wall and inhale deeply. Of all the shit I've gone through in my life, that might have been the worst.

Okay, that didn't go so badly, right? I only have to do that however more thousand times until he ultimately retires. And if luck is on my side, the Kingsmen won't renew his contract for next year. Easy peasy.

three

. . .

Lee

I blink and blink again and look around. Sure as shit, it's not a dream, Shayna is walking out of the room.

Of all the things I expected to deal with this week, coming face-to-face with my biggest regret was not one of them. Seeing her again pulls all that self-esteem out of me and throws it in a garbage disposal because she's a reminder of the slimeball I was with her.

She looks different than she did in college—no glasses, shorter hair that's lighter with a hint of darker roots showing. But she's just as beautiful. And even though she didn't utter a word, she must be just as smart, otherwise, she wouldn't have ended up working for the Kingsmen. Dr. Carlisle and Dr. Frampton are notoriously rigorous in their hiring of new staff.

"Did you know she was working for the team now?" Miles interrupts my thoughts.

I shake my head. "Of course not. What? You think she called me to use me as a reference?"

Miles holds up his hands. "It's odd to just show up. She must've known she'd see you."

"What do you mean?" I look away from the direction Shayna went and over at my best friend.

He gives me a look like I'm an idiot. "Even people who don't follow football know you play for the Kingsmen. She would've too when she applied for and accepted the job."

A small smile tips the corners of my lips because she does follow football. "Maybe she's ready to forgive me."

Miles shrugs and stands, clamping me on the shoulder. "Wouldn't assume that either." I'm busy thinking, and he clears his throat, not walking down the stairs. "Listen, man, you can't let her get in your head."

My eyebrows crinkle. "What? Never." But I already feel my head spinning, unsure how to handle this.

"You say that, but you're forgetting I was your roommate. I saw how the breakup affected you."

I shrug his hand off my shoulder and stand. "Thanks, Dad."

He follows me. "I'm serious, Lee. Don't let her mess up your mental game. It's just as important as the physical one."

We walk down the stairs to exit the auditorium. I hold up my hand to get him to stop talking. "Whatever would I do without you, oh wise one?"

"Probably play for the Canadian Football League."

I shake my head. It's a running joke between us, but Miles knows as well as I do that most of the guys in my home country could play in the NFL. There's just not enough spots for everyone.

Which is why I work my ass off every day to guarantee I'm a part of the league.

In the hallway, I chat with some of the coaching staff about my workouts during the off-season—how I've kept in shape and my diet—then I'm sent to the medical offices to undergo my physical assessment.

A small part of me is excited at the prospect of seeing Shayna day in and day out. She's crossed my mind almost daily over the years and not just because she's the one person I treated the worst in my entire life. Back in college, I got a taste of what we could be together and if I hadn't fucked up, she could be the one I'm going home to tonight instead of an empty condo.

I hope I'm right about her taking a position with the team meaning that she's ready to forgive me and move on. I tried to get her back in college, but after she brushed me off numerous times, ignored me completely, and got angry at me for continuing to approach her, I gave up and stayed away from her for the rest of my time in Michigan.

Sure, I was painfully aware we still shared the same campus because I'd spot her off in the distance sometimes or pass her in the hall or on a pathway through campus, but she'd always look away or sharply turn at the last minute. Each time it happened, I'd lose all focus and it took every ounce of willpower to not chase after her.

But here, she has to work with me. It's my time to make amends.

Miles is right when he says I can't let her fuck with my head. I have a contract renewal coming up at the end of the season, and with our roster, there's a real possibility we could make it deep into the playoffs this year, if not the Super Bowl. I need to put this thing with Shayna to rest sooner than later because it'll hang over my head like a thunderstorm until it's resolved.

I walk into the trainers' room and immediately inspect each athlete and trainer for Shayna. She's off in the corner working with Brady Banks, our new wide receiver we picked up during the off-season.

She's straddling his leg to assess his knee and my fists squeeze together, desperate to unleash my sudden anger. Brady Banks has a reputation in this league. Professionally, the guy is the best there is, which is why he went free agent this year and had multiple teams vying for him. It's his private life reputation that's making jealousy turn my stomach as if he and Shayna are both naked.

Coach told me to report to Dr. Frampton, but instead, my feet move to Banks and Shayna. I tell myself it's because I've been wanting to get to know Brady and what better opportunity than now to invite him out with me this weekend. I mean, he's the guy I'll be throwing to most of the season, so we should get off on the right foot and all.

"Hey, Brady." I put out my hand. "Wanted to come by and say hi."

Shayna's body stiffens and her blueish-green eyes meet mine for the briefest second.

He puts out his hand and we shake. "Hey, man. Good to meet you."

"How are you liking San Fran so far?" I cross my arms and widen my stance, willing Shayna to chime in.

He slyly grins. "These are my old stomping grounds. I grew up here."

"Well, I guess that's why the Kingsmen won you."

"What am I? A stuffed animal in a crane game?"

"You were about that hard to win." We both laugh.

"I hate those fuckers. I never win."

I glance at Shayna, who's stepped away from his legs. Finally, fuck.

"You sure you're not going to miss the Wisconsin winters?" I ask.

He chuckles. "Not even a little."

Shayna pretends she doesn't hear us.

Brady must notice me staring because he gestures toward her. "Have you met Shayna yet? We were just bonding over being the newbies on the team. And the fact she's from Wisconsin. The fans are probably burning my jersey back there."

"They're loyal if nothing else," I say.

She smiles—at him. Of course she does. My jaw tics.

"Hi, Shayna," I say.

She draws in a deep breath and turns her head in my direction. "Nice to meet you." She nods.

The cold and clinical nature of her hello freezes my insides. She's clearly not here to put anything behind us.

So that's how she wants to play it? Pretend we don't know each other? Pretend I haven't been balls deep inside her while she screams my name when she comes? All right, I'll play along. For now that is.

"Same. I hope everyone's been nice."

Her eyes narrow an infinitesimal amount, but I notice. She's trying to act unaffected by my presence. "Everyone's been very nice, yes."

I nod. "Good to hear." Looking back in Brady's direction, I say, "I came over to see if you want to go out on Saturday night. Nothing crazy, just thought we should get to know each other better before the season. But let me make the arrangements. I know you've lived here a while, but I have some killer hookups in the city. I'll work my magic and get back to you."

"Great. Do your thing."

I glance at Shayna one last time. "It was nice to meet you."

She nods but doesn't bother making eye contact with me, instead focusing on stretching out Brady's foot.

I reluctantly walk over to Dr. Frampton. She's clearly still giving me the cold shoulder. Guess that means I'll have to try harder to warm her up. For both of our benefits this season.

four

. . .

Shayna

By the time afternoon hits, the players are out on the practice field. Most of the medical staff observe from the sidelines, keeping an eye out for any sign of weakness or injury that a player either isn't aware of or is trying to hide.

The reality is that there are only so many open spots on the roster and it wouldn't be the first time an athlete on the brink of making it doesn't mention a tight hamstring or a sore knee. Part of our job during training camp is to look for that sort of thing and give input to our superiors. It's all for the betterment of the team, but I feel like a snitch. I would hate to be responsible for someone not achieving their dream.

But the fact number forty-one keeps pulling up his left leg slightly faster than his right, as if it hurts when he bears all his weight on his left knee, isn't what's forefront in my mind.

As much as it irks me, Lee Burrows is consuming my attention.

Partly because I have to stand on the sidelines and watch him practice. It's like I'm at a Chippendales show, because I'm growing hotter the more he sweats. It's abundantly clear that the man is still a football god. It's not like I didn't already know, but seeing it live and in person is another thing altogether. I can't keep my eyes off him long enough to pay attention to the other players. Lee moves around the field with such fluid movement and a commanding presence. Does he really have to lift his shirt to clear the sweat off his face? God, his abs are incredible. My thighs clench together at the remembrance of having him there.

I thought I'd put my attraction and lust for him to rest a long time ago, but apparently not.

I saw that quick flash of hurt in his eyes when he came to talk to Brady while I was working on him. It was a split second—there and gone—but for whatever reason, his expression has stuck with me all day.

When I saw him approach, I thought Lee was going to be all caveman, so I was surprised when he took my sign and pretended we didn't know one another. There's no pleasure on my part in hurting him. I just have to remind my subconscious that we hate Lee Burrows—no matter how hot he makes me.

I force myself to turn my attention elsewhere on the field just before Lee tosses a ball Brady's way.

"It's hard to look away, isn't it?"

I startle at a woman's voice next to me. She's a petite brunette with olive skin, dark eyes, and dark hair to match, wearing tan dress pants and a black mock-neck tank. Must be some bigwig here.

"I'm sorry?"

She gestures toward the field. "It's hard to look away from them, isn't it? They're all at the top of their game, in their prime… all that testosterone needy for somewhere and someone to unleash it on."

I laugh and look at the ID around her neck. The wind has flipped it over, stopping me from reading it. I like to think I'm no longer as shy as I was in college, but I'm still reserved, and she's clearly anything but. Not that she's wrong. These men are the kind who can pick you up and fuck you against a wall without breaking a sweat.

She holds out her hand. "Bryce Burns. I write sports for the *San Jose Chronicle*."

"Good to meet you. Shayna Kudrow. I'm an athletic trainer." I accept her hand.

"You're new."

My cheeks heat. "Is it that obvious?"

She waves me off. "Not at all. I've covered the Kingsmen for the past three years and I would have recognized you."

My shoulders relax. "I just moved here to take this job."

"Good for you. Great opportunity, but still, it's scary, right? At least that's how I felt when I moved to take the job at the *Chronicle*."

"Oh, where were you before you came here?"

"Idaho." Her tone suggests I'd think less of her. "Go ahead with the potato jokes. Don't be shy."

"I won't say potato if you don't ask me about cheese." I raise my hand. "Wisconsin."

She chuckles. "Deal."

I've always liked my home state, but it's true that being surrounded by vast farmland and cows leaves you itching for more. "I take it you like California?"

Her smile transforms her face and makes her eyes sparkle. "Love it. There's so much to see and do. The weather is almost always perfect. I don't even mind the foggy days in the city."

"Do you live around here or are you in San Francisco?"

That was one of the big questions when I moved here— would I live in the San Jose area, closer to the arena and training center, or base myself in nearby San Francisco? I opted, for financial reasons, to live in San Jose. San Francisco rent is insane and I don't want to be scraping by to make ends meet.

"I pay a small fortune to live in San Fran, but it's worth it.

That's where all the action is." She grins, and I'm instantly attracted to her personality and want to be her new best friend. "What about you?"

"I'm in San Jose. Would've liked to be in the city, but then I'd be forced to maintain my college student diet and I enjoy my expensive lattes too much."

She laughs. "I hear you. Believe me. Every month when my rent clears my bank account, I cry."

We both laugh.

She studies me for a moment then says, "What are you doing this weekend?"

My head draws back.

"Any chance you might want to come into the city for some fun?"

I continue to stare at her.

"Why are you looking at me like that?" Her forehead wrinkles.

"Sorry, it's just… you don't even know me. Is this some reporter thing where you befriend me and try to get me to spill dirt on the team?"

We've been warned about talking to the press. If they ask us questions, we have to keep our responses noncommittal and not say anything about any of the athletes' health.

She laughs so hard she's folded over at the waist. When she straightens, she looks at me with a smile. "Not at all. In fact, we don't even have to talk about the team if you don't want. I just figured you're new in town and you probably don't know a lot of people. I remember how lonely I felt." I eye her skeptically, and she holds her hands up in front of her. Damn Lee for making me insecure about people's intentions. "I swear. I have some colleagues I consider acquaintances, but I've never really connected with anyone around my own age since I moved here a few years ago. And I thought you might have the same dilemma here among mostly men." She eyes me and I giggle. "Who knew making friends as adults was so hard? I briefly thought I might need a kid, but I'd be that lady with a baby at a nightclub, grinding."

She's right about that. Dating is hard, but I swear, making friends is even harder.

The tension leaves my body. She's just looking for a friend like I am. "Sure, that sounds like fun."

"Awesome. What's your cell number? I'll add you to my phone and send you the details."

We exchange numbers and a warm feeling spreads through my chest. I'm hopeful I'm on the way to having my first friend in my new hometown. Especially someone as outgoing as Bryce. I need someone to pull me out of my intro-verted ways and force me out of my comfort zone from time to time.

"Perfect." Bryce slides her phone into her cross-body bag. "I'd better go get some quotes, otherwise my editor will have my ass. Looking forward to this weekend."

"Me too."

She gives me a small wave and heads down the field to where some of the players are huddled on the sidelines.

I can't stop smiling. Things are better than I expected for my first day.

"Heads up!" someone screams.

I look to the field where Brady is rushing toward me with his arms out. I step aside as the ball whistles past me.

Brady comes to a stop in front of me. "Sorry, Shayna. Burrows thinks he's on the playground."

Someone behind us tosses him the ball and he jogs back onto the field with it. My gaze goes to Lee, who's staring at me, but I can't make out his expression because of his helmet. Doesn't matter though. That man has epic control of the ball when it leaves his hands, so he threw it in my direction to get my attention. How immature.

Maybe things aren't going as well as I thought.

five

· · ·

Lee

The guys and I meet up at my condo and have a couple of drinks before we head to the nightclub Brady arranged a private table for us at. The man is right, he has connections. He got us into Noveau, the hottest spot in the San Fran

Truth be told, I'd rather be lying on my couch and doing nothing. Training camp is kicking my ass, even with our shortened day today, but I made the plans and I never back out.

Plus, I can never admit that my invitation to Brady had more to do with saving face in front of Shayna than anything else. Not that I was lying. I do need to get to know the guy better and trust him.

The dark SUV drops us off in front of a nondescript building. If it weren't for the long line of people and the low thumping bass emanating from inside, no one would give it a second glance. There's no sign, no advertisement. Just a massive Gothic-looking door with a bunch of bouncers who look like they could be linebackers on the Kingsmen.

"This is Nouveau?" I ask Brady as I slide out onto the sidewalk.

"Yeah. I think it's a play on the term nouveau riche," he says. When my forehead wrinkles, he continues. "Cole Webber owns it. He's like a pseudo uncle to me. His wife is best friends with my stepmom… long story." He waves me off. "Anyway, I think it's sort of like a fuck you to his father because he left the family business and made his own money." Brady shrugs.

Cole Webber is his pseudo uncle? Well, shit. The Webbers own half the restaurants and bars in the Bay area. Cole Webber owns Hard Rock Whiskey, a staple in every club from here to New York.

"Looks like it's doing well." I glance at the long line.

"We're not gonna have to wait in that fucking line, are we?" Chase asks, following my line of vision.

Chase Andrews is the tight end for the Kingsmen, and he's been his usual grumpy self all night.

"No way. Banks hooked us up, didn't you?" Miles clamps him on the shoulder.

"You know it." He nods toward the bouncer.

While they exchange a few words, the people in line start to recognize us and call out our names.

"This is the year, Burrows!"

"Banks is our Golden Ticket!"

"Can I have your number, Miles?"

"Marry me?"

"Who?"

"Any of them," a girl says and the crowd laughs.

We all give a smile and a wave before we're ushered inside by one of the bouncers.

The inside of this place is insane and way bigger than it looks from the outside. The music reverberates in my chest as we walk along the perimeter of the main floor. There's a large dance floor in the middle, and a bar spans the entire back wall. It has to be a hundred feet long. On either side of the room are raised VIP sections, clearly meant for those patrons who want to be seen. Another two VIP levels hang high above. The club lights glisten off the crystal chandelier in the middle of the dance floor, sending colored lights cascading down the walls.

I'm hopeful the bouncer will escort us up to the second or third level, so we won't be on display all night, but he leads us to a VIP section in the middle of the main floor, positioned slightly over the dance floor.

I lean in to Brady. "Can't we get a spot up there?" I point at the balconies above us.

"How are we supposed to talk to the ladies if we're two or three stories above them?" He winks.

I guess Brady's reputation isn't false. He's no stranger to one-night stands. I'd be a hypocrite if I said I was, so there's no judgment from me. But after being in proximity with Shayna all week, I don't want some random woman in my bed. I want her.

Right now, she's the only woman I think about, but thinking about her makes me remember I'm the world's biggest asshole. If only I could have the opportunity to convey to her how sorry I am. I need her to forgive me and understand that what we had had nothing to do with the bet. What happened between us has always hung over my head and this has to be some sign that it's time to make amends.

A bottle waitress, dressed appropriately for her job with all her assets hanging out for guys to ogle, saunters over to take our order. She pretends she doesn't know us, which is ridiculous because either the bouncer or the manager informed her exactly who we are. But acting as though she doesn't know us must be her thing and I'm not one to broadcast myself. Ten minutes later, she returns with the bottles we requested.

After she's poured our drinks, we sit on the couches. I'm seated beside Brady while Miles and Chase are on the couch across from us, looking bored as fuck.

For Miles, I get it. Nightclubs have never been his scene. He's always in for a good time, but he's not looking for a party girl who will either out him on social or try to hook her claws in him. One day he'll settle down with some agreeable woman who likes going to the theater and playing Scrabble on a Saturday night.

Chase is just a grumpy fuck. He's scowling at the dance floor as if every individual out there has personally offended him. The bar scene is more his thing. At some point tonight, we'll lose track of him either because he took a woman home or he went to his usual bar that's just down the street from here.

Brady looks as though he's just arrived at heaven and it's as great as he's heard it is. He's leaning back on the couch, the arm opposite me spread wide while he eye-fucks some of the women who are dancing provocatively in an attempt to get us to notice them. They clearly know who we are.

I lean over so Brady will hear me over the music. "So, you're single, right?"

He barely glances in my direction, not taking his eyes off the women. "What gave it away?" He chuckles.

I laugh.

He sips his drink. "I'm not into anything serious. Being a dad is stressful as fuck, so a good lay and a few drinks with the boys tonight sounds good."

"I heard you were a single dad. That's a big load with an NFL career, too?"

An athlete as high profile as Brady Banks doesn't have a lot of privacy. Although I don't know details, I do know he's a single dad. Which probably gets him even more ladies.

He grabs his phone from the glass table in front of us, showing me his screensaver. Smiling at me is a sandy-haired boy with hazel eyes. Almost an exact replica of Brady.

"This is Theo. He's five, and the most important thing in my life."

"He's cute." I sip my drink. "The mom?"

He shakes his head and returns his phone to the table. "One-night stand. But Hannah is great. We tried to make it work at first, but we're better off as friends."

I nod slowly. I can't imagine being responsible for another human being. "Does she live in San Francisco?"

He blows out a breath and nods. "When I got picked up by the Kingsmen, she didn't balk at all about picking up her life and moving to San Francisco. We always try to do what's best for Theo, and we need to live in the same city for him."

My eyes widen. "Wow. That's decent of her."

He nods while taking another sip of his drink. "She always puts Theo first. Plus, she just took a job as a travel nurse, so it doesn't matter as much where her home base is. Still, she could've easily told me to go fuck myself when I asked if she'd consider moving to California with me. I admire any woman who puts her kid ahead of herself."

It feels like there's something more behind his statement than he's letting on, but I don't pry. "If she's a travel nurse, does that mean she's away from home a lot?"

He shakes his head. "She mostly takes assignments when I'm in the off-season, and the ones she takes while I'm in season are usually short ones—like a few days or so. But now that I'm back in my hometown, I have my dad, my stepmom, and my siblings to help out when necessary."

"Sounds like the Kingsmen was the perfect fit."

He chuckles and shakes his head. "Pretty much."

Brady flashes me a mischievous smile, then looks back at all the women on the dance floor. He must see something that interests him because he stands, slides his phone in his pants, and walks over to the railing.

Miles motions me over, so I grab my drink and walk around the table to him and Chase, but they both stand from the couch at the same time.

"I know Banks set this whole thing up, but how long do I have to stay?" Miles asks.

"Why don't you try relaxing, drink a few drinks, and have a good time?" I arch an eyebrow.

"This just isn't my scene," he bites out.

"Cavanaugh forgot to bring his book." Chase hits Miles in the chest, and although Miles looks ready to tackle Chase, I can't stifle my laugh.

Miles rolls his eyes at Chase. "You're telling me you're having a good time?"

Chase scoffs. "Hell no. What the hell am I gonna do with one of these chicks?"

"Make them cry," Miles says.

Chase isn't known for subtlety, and we've seen more than a few women in tears over the years.

"We all need to get to know Banks better. It'll help us be a team on the field." I raise my drink to my lips.

Chase rolls his eyes. "Fine. But if I have to stay here and listen to this shitty electronic music all night, then you owe me, Burrows."

"Christ, I'm never getting out of here." Miles pushes a hand through his dark curls and throws himself on the couch. My attention is drawn to him scowling at the dance floor.

I follow Miles's line of vision. Brady is still leaning over the railing separating the VIP section from the dance floor, talking to a woman below. I can't tell if I know her because his body is blocking my view. But I can perfectly make out the woman standing to the right of the woman and see why Miles acted like a toddler.

Shayna.

And Jesus, she puts every other woman here to shame. She's curled her hair wavy and loose, falling just past her shoulders. Her black fitted dress leaves nothing to the imagination as it dips low enough to show off her cleavage. Her red lipstick makes my dick twitch. What those lips would feel like wrapped around my cock.

"What's the story there?" Chase asks.

"Later," I say.

"She went to college with us," Miles informs him. "They have unfinished business."

"I'll gladly take her off your hands." I scowl at Chase and he holds up his hands. "Hell, I'm kidding. I have rules. I don't sleep with women I work with or women related to my friends. I like my love life to be clear and simple."

"You probably make them sign NDAs." Miles's eyebrows rise.

There have been rumors, but no one has the guts to ask Chase. When Miles gets pissy, he gets ballsy like he wants a fight.

"Do I look like the type?" Chase asks.

Miles and I both appraise him.

"Yeah," we say in unison, and he shakes his head, taking a drink.

Brady is talking to the bouncer, and soon enough, Shayna and who I now see is that reporter from the *Chronicle*, Bryce, are coming up into the VIP section. My heart races and a sweat—not from how fucking hot it is in here—beads along my forehead.

I approach Shayna, but she glides right past me and sits on the couch. "How are things, Miles?"

Miles is shocked, stumbling on an answer, and Chase soaks in the scene with amusement, laughing his ass off.

Fucker.

six

. . .

Shayna

My mind must be playing tricks on me, because I could swear I heard my name being called. Then again, between the drinks Bryce insisted we have before we left her place and what I've had since we got here, I'm slightly tipsy.

I felt out of place the minute the bouncers allowed us entry and I found out the tight dress Bryce forced me to change into—because apparently my dress pants and silk tank top wouldn't cut it for Noveau, the newest and hottest nightclub in San Francisco—was apparently the appropriate uniform for this place.

When I hear my name a second time, I look over my shoulder and find Brady Banks leaning over the railing from one of the VIP sections, waving us over to him.

Shit. I swore the players were bound to some curfew, so I never thought we'd run into any of them here. Great second impression. I'm drunk and wearing a dress that could be used as Saran Wrap.

Then the question dings in my mind. Who is he here with? I remember Lee asking Brady to go out while I was working on Brady and Brady saying he'd hook them up.

I motion for Bryce to follow me and push my way through

the few people separating us from the VIP section. Brady's million-dollar smile doesn't distract me from looking over his shoulder at Lee, Miles, and Chase on the couches.

Quadruple shit.

I like Brady. This entire week, he's seemed like a nice guy who lives for his son. And he's new to the team, so I can't hold the company he keeps against him.

We say polite hellos and chat for a minute, but his attention turns to Bryce, who is dancing in place. I understand why. First off, Bryce is single, available, and gorgeous. Second, she's got that outgoing personality that garners attention everywhere she goes. Third, she doesn't work for the Kingsmen.

I dutifully ignore the men behind Brady, but it doesn't stop me from feeling the searing sensation of Lee's gaze. He's making this whole situation so much worse. Eventually we'll have to talk and be cordial, otherwise it'll be a very long year—or longer, if he doesn't change teams.

I breathe a sigh of relief when Brady walks away—we can go back onto the dance floor and disappear into the crowd now. But they must have come to an agreement, because Brady talks to a bouncer and Bryce slides her arm through mine, leading me over to the roped-off area. Please say it isn't so.

Bryce smiles at me as though we're so lucky, unaware of the history between Lee and myself. "Brady invited us to join him. Come on."

She tightens her arm in mine and drags me toward the bouncer, whose job is to keep girls like us from boys like them unless they say it's okay.

"I probably shouldn't," I shout, hoping she can hear me. "I mean... I work with them."

She doesn't change course or stop until we're in front of the bouncer. When she faces me, I half wonder if she sees how pale I probably am from the nauseous feeling in my stomach that has nothing to do with the alcohol we've drunk.

"You can still hang out with them. You just can't go home with any of them." She laughs at what a preposterous idea she thinks that is, and I pretend to find enjoyment in it as well.

"Um…"

She sticks out her bottom lip like a pouty child. "Come on. Brady seems really nice."

She smiles like a girl who sees a glimmer of hope for her romantic future, whether just tonight or forever, and my stomach sinks because I'm not going to say no to her. I get the appeal. I was her once.

Plus, Bryce has taken me under her wing and befriended me in a new town where I know no one. And I like her and see where a friendship could blossom between us. What is one night, a few hours? I can handle that. Plus, Miles was always easy to talk to.

As the bouncer's hand moves to the metal clasp to unhook the rope that blocks off the set of stairs leading up to Lee, my stomach spins and my heart hammers. The bouncer motions us forward and I can barely put one foot in front of the other, thinking of an excuse to flee that Bryce would believe.

"Hey," I say, putting my hand on Bryce's, but I'm too late.

Brady greets us at the top stair with that crazy gorgeous smile that has earned him plenty of women in his bed.

"Shayna." He wraps his arms around me as though we're long-lost childhood friends. "This is a different look for you." He's not looking at me as though he wants to throw me over his shoulder and run out of the club, which is good.

I pretend to be confident in a dress that would never hang in my closet—especially if I thought I'd run into the guys I work with and only want to view me as a professional. Not a party girl with her tits on display. So I'm thankful Brady doesn't give the same vibe most guys on the dance floor were.

"I didn't think leggings and a T-shirt would work tonight," I say.

He laughs. "Definitely a better option." His eyes travel down Bryce and back up, the two sharing a look that causes me to imagine the two of them in a situation I don't want to. "And you look gorgeous."

Bryce's smile could light up the entire San Francisco skyline.

"Come on over to our table." He circles around and makes his way past the other tables, and men and women gawk and point and whisper as he passes. It says something about you when the VIPs are admiring the fellow VIPs.

The other three sit on two couches, all eyes on us.

"Why is Miles Cavanaugh looking at you like you shot his childhood pet?" I whisper to Bryce.

She rolls her eyes. "Because I call him out in my articles when he plays like shit. Apparently he has a fragile ego."

I stifle a laugh. Miles didn't strike me as having a fragile anything back in college. Regardless, it's clear from the sneer he's giving Bryce that there's no love lost between them.

When we reach the table, Brady stops and motions at the two of us behind him. "Look who I found."

Whereas I'm uncomfortable with Brady, Chase, and Miles seeing me in this dress, I couldn't be happier about Lee's eyes devouring me as though he wants to whisk me away into a corner. I just wish I didn't want him to.

It's bad enough the hunger in his eyes sends a frisson of electricity racing through me. I want to torture him, not myself.

The guys all say hello, and Brady sits next to Bryce. Both Miles and Chase are seated on one couch, leaving only Lee and myself standing.

He steps to approach me, but I walk right by him and sit next to Miles. "How are things, Miles?"

Chase laughs and Lee shoots him a death glare.

Brady mixes Bryce and me a drink, and when the cold glass meets my palm, I take a huge swig. My buzz has completely worn off.

"Burrows?" Brady asks, because Lee is still standing, looking as if he's contemplating squeezing in beside me rather than taking the free spot across from me.

He looks at Brady.

"You going somewhere?" Brady asks.

Lee's eyebrows furrow for a moment. Bryce and Chase laugh as Miles shakes his head.

"No." Lee sits on the couch opposite me, next to Brady and Bryce.

For a moment, Miles's gaze is fixated on Brady and Bryce talking, but he strips his eyes from them and turns to me. "How are you liking your new job so far?"

I nod and lean in so he can hear me. "It's good. It's taken a minute to learn the team dynamics and how Dr. Carlisle and Dr. Frampton prefer things done, but I think I have a lot figured out now."

"Carlisle's an asshole," Chase blurts. His arms are crossed and he's leaning back into the couch, staring at the dance floor. I didn't think he was listening to us.

"Maybe, but he's the best there is. You guys are lucky to have him." Shit. Now I know the alcohol has loosened my lips. Otherwise I would never shit talk my boss with the players.

My discomfort must show on my face because Chase sighs.

"Relax. I'm not some schoolgirl who's gonna go tattle," Chase says.

"Thanks."

I quickly keep up the conversation as a distraction. Chase mostly grunts here and there to indicate he's paying attention, but Miles and I hold a conversation about how I got from the University of Michigan to California.

About ten minutes in, Chase says, "Gotta take a piss." He stands and walks away.

Miles looks at Chase and shakes his head. "Don't let his attitude bother you." Then he glances in the direction I won't dare. "He's staring, giving me a look that he wants to take me to the alley and beat the shit out of me." He smiles and slides a little closer to me.

I don't want to look, but I know Miles is right. Lee is making this entire interaction uncomfortable. Does he think I can't feel his eyes on me? I glance at the couch across from us, and the intensity of Lee's stare could scorch me. We're talking in hushed tones, and over the music, there's no way Lee can hear us.

"He's going to blow his top soon." Miles looks at me from the corner of his eye.

I shake my head. "You had a lot of offers. Why did you come to the Kingsmen?"

I've wondered when he got traded and heard a lot of teams wanted him. Did he come here because of Lee?

"Lee," he says. "I know there's lost love between you two, or I guess just you, but I love the fucker. And speaking of the fucker, I give us about two more minutes before he stomps over here."

I push aside him suggesting that Lee would still want me. That is not something I need floating around in my head. "And whatever happened to McKenzie?"

He laughs, but a motion in our peripheral grabs his attention. He laughs harder. "Here he comes."

Miles is just about to tell me something when a lean, muscular body drops into the seat between us, wiggling his hips for each of us to slide over and make room.

Not granting Miles any attention, Lee turns his back on his friend to face me.

"Excuse me, but Miles and I were in the middle of something." I gesture beyond Lee toward his best friend.

"Yeah, I'm out." Miles stands and walks out of the VIP lounge. Of course he has Lee's back.

Lee scoffs. "It can't be as important as what we need to discuss."

"There's nothing to discuss, Lee. We said everything we had to say to each other years ago."

His back straightens. "Hardly. You shut the door in my face and cut off all communication." His knee brushes my bare thigh and a million volts of energy explode inside me.

"All right, correction. I said everything I needed to say." I bring my glass to my lips and take a heavy pull on the straw.

Lee studies my profile while I attempt to appear relaxed, bopping to the music as though I can't imagine anywhere else I'd rather be, even though the opposite is true.

After a few minutes, he says, "You look so different."

My head whips in his direction. "So you're saying I either looked like shit in college or I do now?"

He scoffs. "Not at all. You know I thought you were hot as fuck back then and it's the same now."

I tilt my head in a placating gesture. "Sure. Making me believe that you thought I was hot was part of the bet."

His jaw sets and twitches. "You don't just look different. You are different. You're more… confident, outspoken. It's good. Though I did really love my shy pie."

I stiffen at the pet name he gave me in college. "Don't," I grind out between clenched teeth.

"Don't what?"

"Don't call me that."

"Shy pie? Why not? You used to like the nickname." He downs a healthy gulp of his drink and sets it on the table in front of us.

My eyes narrow. "Pet names are reserved for people who

like each other. And I don't know if you've noticed or not, but I'm not part of the Lee Burrows fan club anymore."

"You used to be fucking president."

I suck in a breath from the longing in his voice. He spoke the words as if he'd do anything to travel back to that time.

Well, too bad. He made his bed.

"I think I'm going to go to the restroom." I signal to Bryce that I'm going to go to the bathroom.

Like the girl's girl I thought she was, she starts to stand to come with me, but I wave her off and head out of the VIP lounge without a backward glance, only too happy to get some distance from the man who still makes my pulse race.

seven

. . .

Lee

Shayna stomps off and I fail at trying not to stare at the way her dress clings to her ass. It took a Herculean effort not to let my gaze dip to her cleavage when she was sitting beside me.

Miles returns and watches Shayna leave. He shakes his head and sits. "You're completely screwed."

"What are you talking about?"

He nods in the direction Shayna took off in. "You're still hung up on her."

I stare toward the hallway of the bathrooms, wanting to run over to them, lock her in a stall, and make her hear my side of the story. "I am not. I just need her to know I'm not the loser she thinks I am. That the bet in college had nothing to do with what transpired between us afterward."

Miles doesn't smile and his eyes leave mine when Bryce laughs at something Brady says. "Who cares what she thinks of you if you're not into her anymore?" He smirks with his eyebrows raised because the fucker knows me too well.

"I can't explain it. It's just… it's the worst thing I've ever done to anybody and I need her to know I'm not the guy she thinks."

He clasps my knee. "Good luck with it. Like I said —screwed."

He doesn't understand, but then why would he? Miles hails from a nice Midwest family with married parents, a sister, a golden retriever, and a literal white picket fence. He didn't grow up with a mom who couldn't get out of bed in the morning due to her depression over her husband's early death. He didn't feel like a constant disappointment.

That's got to be why I'm so desperate to make her see that what we had meant so much to me.

She probably assumes I'm trying to get into her pants, but she's wrong. Am I still attracted to her? Hell yes. But the last thing I need is to get all twisted up the way I was after shit went down with us. I was a mess and would probably have blown my scholarship if my brother Kane hadn't calmed me down. My life is the same now as it was then. I still have too much on the line. I need to focus on my job and be the best damn quarterback in the league, proving my worth so I can secure the contract I want at the end of the season. And there's no way I'll be successful at that if I allow myself to be in a relationship with Shayna.

"I'll be back in a minute," I tell Miles.

"Advice?" he yells after me.

I put up my hand. "NO!"

"Where is Burrows going?" Brady asks before I'm out of earshot.

"To get his balls kicked."

Brady laughs and asks for clarification, but I trust Miles won't say anything.

The bathrooms are unisex, a series of small individual rooms down a long hallway. I wait at the end of the line of doors since I'm not sure which one Shayna is in. Regardless, she'll have to pass me to return to our section, so she won't escape me.

Knowing Chase, he took off and is probably at his local bar by now. It wouldn't be the first time.

Shayna darts out of a doorway near the end of the hall a minute later. She's oblivious to me, searching her purse as she walks my way. I see the moment she realizes that I'm waiting. Her feet lose their cadence, irritation coats her features, and she blows out a long breath.

"What do you want?" She stops in front of me with her arms crossed, hip cocked.

Not knowing if I'll ever see her dressed like this again, I let my gaze trail down to the deep *V* of her dress so I can soak in the view of her cleavage. I pretend not to notice the way her nipples pebble under the thin fabric when she quickly drops her arms to her sides, figuring—rightly—that crossing her arms would only make her tits more pronounced.

"I want to talk to you."

"I have nothing to say." She pushes past me, but I take her upper arm, pulling her into a dark dead-end hallway with a set of doors. With her back against the wall, she rips her arm from my hold. "Jesus, Lee."

I hold up my hands. "Give me five minutes?"

She huffs but doesn't walk away. I take that as my sign.

"Shayna, I need you to know that I've thought a lot about what went down between us over the years."

A sly smirk lifts one corner of her lips. "Feeling guilty all this time? Good."

I step closer to her and she steps back to maintain the distance between us, except she has nowhere to go, so I step back so as not to crowd her.

"Yes. But not because I lied to you about my feelings. Because I didn't tell you about the bet before I let anything happen between us."

"What do you want from me?" She throws her hands in the air.

"I want you to forgive me. I want you to believe me." I

search her face for any indication that she's ready to leave the past in the past, but I see none.

"Fine. You're forgiven. Can I go back to the table now?"

My fists clench. "You're so stubborn."

"Well, I've been hurt many times in my life and I don't tend to give second chances for people to hurt me again."

"What will it take for you to believe me?" Our eyes lock and I step forward.

She tries to sidestep but ends up in a corner. "Once a liar, always a liar." Her hands are splayed on the wall behind her.

"Believe me, I wanted to tell you. But I was afraid it would ruin what we had started. When I made that bet, I didn't know you. How much I would fall head over heels for you. And since I never really had any intention of going through with the bet after sleeping with you… I don't know. I guess I foolishly convinced myself it wasn't that big a deal if I didn't tell you."

"Omission is still a lie."

My hands fly out to my sides. "I was just a poor punk-ass kid who didn't have a dime to his name. I made the bet to get my truck fixed, not knowing that I'd be entering my first real relationship that would matter to me. My decision-making was not stellar and if I had a crystal ball…"

Her face softens slightly, but it's gone in an instant. "You hurt me and embarrassed me."

I groan her name and lift my arms so that my palms are spread on the wall on either side of her face. I take my chances by stepping closer. "Please. You have no idea, all these years, how terrible I've felt. Forgive me and put me out of my misery."

Our eyes lock and our shared space fills with tension. My gaze dips to her full lips, painted red, and my cock twitches as I remember how soft her lips were when we'd kiss.

She might still be pissed at me, but our bodies still react to each other the same way they did then.

The music vanishes from my awareness. All I hear is our breathing, and as she takes in a quick breath, her chest heaves. God, maybe Miles is right, because I want her forgiveness, but if she asked to go back to my place right now, I'd have her out the back door of this place and in a car before she could change her mind.

But even if she forgave me and even if I was in a place to pursue a relationship, we work together now. That would be completely unprofessional on both of our parts.

But the way she's looking at me with heavy eyelids and her mouth slightly open is like a siren's song. I lean in unconsciously.

Her tongue glides along her bottom lip and her head tilts back as our mouths inch closer to one another's. My eyes drift closed moments before my lips will land on hers. I've waited so many years to taste her again and my dick stirs with anticipation. As I'm about to enter heaven, two hands land on my chest and shove me back.

My eyes snap open and Shayna slips under my arm, stomping away without a word.

Fuck, she doesn't forgive me and I have a half-hard dick now. Things couldn't get worse.

eight

. . .

Shayna

The next morning, I wake up on Bryce's lush couch with only a mild throb in my head.

I'm thankful. Given the amount of booze I drank last night, I'm surprised I didn't throw up. But it was the only thing that kept me from spiraling after Lee confronted me in the hallway and we almost shared a kiss. Talk about my vagina being a traitor.

Women don't want to kiss a man they hate.

Truth is, I'm more mad at myself than I am at him. Because that's the kind of behavior I'd expect from the league's top quarterback. I'm sure he's used to getting what he wants when he wants it and never being denied. But I'm the one he screwed over and there should be no room for me to feel anything other than repulsion when I look at him.

If only that were the case.

"Good morning, sunshine."

Bryce's voice causes me to roll over. She's sitting in the chair opposite me, reading on her iPad.

"You're way too chipper for how late we were out last night."

She chuckles. "I'm a morning person. I take it you're not?"

I slowly pull myself into a seated position. "Not if I've been drinking. Thanks for letting me crash here by the way."

I'd planned not to drink so much and figured I'd drive back to San Jose last night, but that plan went to shit once I saw Lee. Bryce had insisted I stay and listed all these things we could do during a sleepover. Needless to say, the alcohol changed those plans too.

"Of course. Now we can go out for brunch and have some mimosas." She grins and wiggles.

I chuckle, undoing the messy bun at the top of my head and redoing it.

"Now…" She leans forward and sets her iPad on the coffee table. "Do you want to tell me now or later?" She crosses her legs and rests her elbows on her knees and her head in her hands.

"What?" I ask. Did I do something really embarrassing last night?

"Are you going to tell me what the deal is between you and Lee Burrows?"

I try to school my face, but her smirk makes it clear I'm not successful. "I don't know what you're talking about."

She scoffs. "Please, after you went to the bathroom, Lee followed and I had to search you out on the dance floor. And there you stayed until it was time to go."

I cover my face with the blanket.

"Oh, this must be good."

I peek from under the blanket and she's rubbing her hands together like an evil sorceress.

I let my head fall forward and meet her gaze. "Is this Bryce the reporter asking or Bryce the friend?"

Her expression turns serious and she straightens her back. "Friend. You have my word that nothing personal you ever tell me will make it into one of my stories. I'd never do that to my new best friend."

We've only just met, but something about Bryce tells me I

can trust her. But… I've been wrong about people before. Lee is the perfect example. Still, it would be nice to have a girl-friend to confide in. Especially because this situation between Lee and me is not going away.

Truthfully, if it ever got out, Lee is the one who would look like the asshole, not me.

So I go into the entire story of what happened between us in college—how I had to tutor him in biology and that I'd always had a crush on him even though we'd never spoken until that point. How he made a move on me, and the rela-tionship I thought was evolving over the weeks. How he made me think that us sleeping together would be the begin-ning of something amazing, only for me to find out he'd made a thousand-dollar bet with his teammate about scoring with me.

Her mouth hangs open. "What a pig!"

"Right? And he wonders why I won't just up and forgive him."

She leans back in her chair and pulls her legs up to her chest. "You're a better woman than I am. I would've strung him up by his balls."

I laugh. "If we'd known each other in college, I would've let you."

"Well, we're best friends now and I promise that any guy who does you dirty will have to answer to me from this point forward."

"Ditto. Now, it's your turn. Are you going to tell me what's going on with you and Brady?" I waggle my eyebrows.

She waves me off. "I thought I might be interested in him for a hot second."

I chuckle. "Sure. What's not to like… he's successful, a professional athlete, totally hot, killer body…"

She arches an eyebrow. "I could say the same about Lee."

Heat rises to my cheeks. "Touché."

We're quiet for a moment, each of us deep in our thoughts.

"So what made you change your mind about him?" I ask.

"I think he's more into getting into my pussy than actually developing a relationship. I've been there and done that. I'm not big on one-night stands anymore."

I nod since I've never been big into one-night stands. But then again, I rarely go to places where I could pick men up like that anyway.

"It did get a little cold for a second when Miles was there." I laugh.

Bryce rolls her eyes. "He pisses me off. So what if he doesn't love everything I write about him? I'm fair—I've said plenty of good as well as bad."

"It surprises me, you know… he was Lee's roommate and best friend in college. I was only in their orbit for a few months and I've only been with the team for a week, but he's never struck me as someone who would get butt hurt about a bad article."

"Or two. Okay, maybe three." She chuckles.

"I guess you just bring out the worst in him." Shrugging, I stand from the couch.

"Maybe. Or maybe he just has a fragile ego and a lot of false bravado." She smacks her hands on her thighs and rises from the chair. "Ready to make ourselves look respectable and grab some brunch?"

"Definitely."

I smile at her and follow her down the hall to her bedroom to change into the clothes I'd originally planned to wear out last night.

Bryce is like the rainbow after a storm. If things go south in California, she'll be my silver lining.

———

By the time I return to my apartment, it's late afternoon. I want nothing more than to veg out on my couch all night, but I need to get a workout in. Not just to clear my mind of Lee Burrows, but because my job is to keep professional athletes healthy, conditioned, and in shape. I'd be a hypocrite if I didn't do the same.

My cell phone rings as I'm changing, and Aunt Suzie's name lights up the screen. I smile at the phone in my hand. My aunt and I have always been close—she was like a second mother to me when I was growing up.

"Hi, Aunt Suzie."

"Hey, you! How's California? How's your job?"

I've been texting with her throughout the week in the rare times I have free time, but I'd promised I'd give her a full update this weekend. "My one boss is still intense, but I'm starting to get the flow of things, I think."

"And how about those players? They treating you well? Do I need to fly out there and kick anyone's ass?"

I chuckle as the image of being caged in Lee's arms last night at the club comes to mind, but I push it away. "All the players have been very welcoming. No worries there."

I never told my aunt what happened between Lee and me. At the time, I was too embarrassed to admit it, and as the years passed, I just wanted to forget my momentary lapse of judgment. It seemed easier than asking myself why I was still giving him any thought at all so many years later.

My aunt asks a few more questions and I give her more details of what I've been up to all week, then she catches me up on some of the more colorful characters she's had come into the restaurant she waits tables at.

"I want you to know how proud I am of you," she says when our conversation comes to a natural lull.

Her words make me smile. "You may have mentioned that a time or two." Or hundred.

"I mean it, Shayna. You're out there doing it on your own,

supporting yourself and making a life for yourself. I'm jealous."

My chuckle is strained because she's not saying the words in jest.

It's no secret that my aunt is in an unhappy marriage. She has been for as long as I can remember. It became obvious to me when I was a teenager. When I asked her about it once—thanks, teenage bravado—rather than denying it and insisting everything was fine, she actually told me the truth.

Maybe it was because I wasn't technically her daughter. I've never talked to her two children, my cousins, about it, so I have no idea if they know, but I've always suspected they must since they grew up in the household.

"I'm sorry." It's all I can think of to say.

"Oh, sweetie, I don't begrudge you the life you're living. Not at all. It's just if I could do it over… you know… I'd do things differently. Not get married so young."

My aunt and uncle were married right out of high school and started a family right away. From her telling, it became clear a few years into the marriage that they weren't suited for each other. My uncle is often gruff, disinterested, and says hurtful things. Over the years, my aunt is pretty sure he's had affairs, but she never confronts him.

She's always felt stuck because she doesn't have a postsecondary education and had three kids to raise. How would she support herself if she left him? What if he didn't pay child support? It was a risk she wasn't willing to take for her children, so instead, she focused on her family and raising her kids.

Watching someone you love live an existence like that is painful, but I took it as a lesson—and so I kept my focus on my studies and excelling at school. I support myself and work my dream job. No matter what, I'll always be able to rely on myself.

"I know you wish you could do things over, but there's

still time to make a change." I grip the phone a little tighter, anticipating her response.

"Not for an old gal like me."

I frown. "You're not that old, Aunt Suzie."

She chuckles. "I appreciate the optimism. Now, what are you doing with the rest of your day?"

"I'm going to head to the gym to get a workout in, then come home and veg out on the couch for the rest of the night. I have to be at work early tomorrow."

"I'll leave you to it then. Let's chat next week, okay?"

"Definitely. You take care of yourself."

"I always do. Bye, sweetie."

We hang up and I sit for a moment, melancholy that my aunt won't even consider leaving my uncle. I just want her to be happy.

Giving my head a shake, I head into my bedroom to change into some workout clothes.

One of the perks of being a trainer for the Kingsmen is that I'm allowed to use the gym when the team isn't training. So once I change, I head down to my car to take the short drive over to the facility, looking forward to pushing Lee Burrows far from my mind.

nine

. . .

Lee

I drop the weights on the floor and heave out a sigh.

The trainers would likely bark at me for being here and overdoing my workouts, but I need to get rid of this tension filling every one of my veins since my altercation with Shayna.

It's a pattern from my youth. After my dad died, any time my mom would slip into a depressive episode, I used physical exhaustion to clear my head and help me sleep.

Maybe I have my mom's mental illness to thank for me becoming a professional athlete. Perhaps if I hadn't had an absentee mother for the majority of my childhood, I wouldn't be where I am today. Hell, she raised, and I use that word loosely, two professional athletes.

I chuckle at that thought and head over to the treadmills. Cardio usually does the trick. It doesn't take long before I go from a jog to a full-out run. I take my job seriously, and being at the peak of my physical fitness is a big part of the job. I'm the quarterback, the captain of the team, which means I set the example for the other players.

Ten minutes into my run, my shirt is soaked through with sweat. I glance up at my reflection in the mirror and lose my footing. My other foot tries to recover so I don't fall, but I'm too preoccupied. I end up running too fast and falling right off—at Shayna's feet. Her arms are crossed and there's a sour look on her face.

I stand to hopefully regain some dignity. A quick look at her in the mirror as I turn off the treadmill shows her biting her lip to stop herself from laughing. I lift my shirt and dry off my sweat-covered face and her smile quickly diminishes. Sexual tension fills the large space.

"What are you doing here?" she snips, stomping off to the treadmill at the very end of the row of machines.

I decide to act as though nothing is amiss with the two of us. Like she's just the new trainer for Kingsmen. Maybe if I stop focusing on the past, we'll eventually move into the future on better footing.

"Working out. Same as you, I imagine."

Her aqua eyes meet mine in the mirror. "I'm surprised you're here."

Is she trying to bait me? Well, if she is, it's not going to work. "Why's that?"

She shrugs and steps up on the treadmill. Her ass looks amazing in a snug pair of yoga pants. "You have a sure spot on the team. You don't need to put in the extra work."

"I'm where I am *because* I put in the extra work." I've witnessed too many athletes who think they've made it and don't need to do anything other than the bare minimum. And then they get cut the next season, or traded.

Xavier Greene is the example I try to emulate.

I was the number two quarterback on the team until he retired, and even though he left at the top of his game, I witnessed firsthand how much harder he worked with each passing year just to keep up the standard he'd set for himself.

Retirement is an inevitability for me, I know. But at twenty-nine, I'm hoping to push off Father Time for at least a few more years—minimum.

Our eyes meet in the mirror again and something passes between us—a mix of longing and regret—and I get the distinct impression she wants to put everything behind us. Or wishes she could, maybe.

Then she pulls her thin, athletic shirt over her head, revealing a sports bra that shows off her ample tits and stomach. I'm reduced to a Neanderthal brain and all I want to do is strip her naked and fuck her against the wall.

I grab the towel and run it down my face as a stall tactic, hoping that covering my eyes will calm me. I'm not going to earn Shayna's forgiveness by ogling her every time she's wearing hardly any clothes.

A part of me wonders why I even care so much. I have the life I've always wanted. And yeah, I screwed her over back in the day, but everyone makes mistakes when they're young and dumb. It's part of growing up and learning and maturing. If she can't forgive me, I should be able to say "fuck it" and move on and forgive myself.

But I can't. For whatever reason, I *need* Shayna to forgive me. Okay, yeah, there's something deeper there. She's the last woman I thought could be something. Someone who wanted me for me and not my status. But I can't have her even if she forgives me. We work together now, and Shayna would never put herself in that position.

"Lee?"

Shayna snaps me back to the here and now.

"Sorry, yeah?" I push my hand through my sweaty hair and don't miss the way her gaze tracks to my bicep.

"I asked if you're here every night."

I cock an eyebrow. "Why? Looking to avoid me?"

She rolls her eyes. "No. I asked because if you are, you're likely overworking your muscles. You'll be doing enough in training camp these next couple of weeks. You should use the time in between to let your body rest."

Bringing my hand to my heart, I tilt my head. "Aw,

listening to you just now, I'd almost think you cared." My sarcasm stems from my previous thought—she can't be mine even if she forgives me. I tend to be a sour asshole when I don't get what I want.

All expression drops from her face. "It's my job to ensure you're in peak physical condition so that you can do your job. Nothing more." The bite in her tone turns me on.

"And what do you think?" I lift my shirt over my head in one fluid motion. "Am I in peak physical form?" Yeah, I'm a class *A* asshole. I need to let this go.

Her gaze drags down my chest and her nipples harden beneath the thin material of her sports bra.

"You're an ass." She hops up onto the treadmill, her finger pressing hard to start it, and starts running, effectively stopping our conversation.

Which is fine. Because at least now I know I can still get to her. It's a start.

But a start to what, jerkoff? You honestly think Shayna's willpower will wane and she'll sleep with you in the gym because you have a set of abs? Get real.

———

Although I'd been at the gym for an hour before Shayna showed up, I extend my workout and go back through all the machines so that I can get little glimpses of her.

I don't like the idea of her being here all by herself at night. And I definitely don't like the idea of her being here alone with another player. Even though that's unlikely at this point.

She's right about overdoing the workouts though. Training camp kicks our asses, and most guys are in bed or playing video games in their off time. And I have no business acting like some jealous lover, but this is the most alone time

I've gotten with her since I found out she was in San Francisco.

I don't talk to her or bother her. She has her earbuds in, but I keep an eye on her so when she walks toward her bag and picks up the shirt she came in wearing, I figure she must be wrapping up her workout.

I stop midlift and put the barbell back, finishing as well. I toss my towel in the dirty hamper next to the locker room and quickly switch my shoes. She's a helluva lot faster than me though and already has her bag hanging from her shoulder.

I call out to her before she reaches the door. "Shayna, wait up."

She turns around with a scowl as though I just told her that her ass doesn't look good in her leggings. Side note—it looks bitable.

"I'll walk you to your car." I break the distance between us with my gym bag slung over my shoulder.

"I'm a big girl. I don't need you to walk me to my car."

"Listen, I get that you're still pissed at me, but I wouldn't let *any* woman walk to her car alone in the dark."

She studies me for a beat and turns around without saying a word. I follow her. The two of us say good night to Paul, the security guard, and we step out into the dark parking lot.

Shayna presses her key fob and the lights of a dark-blue sedan go off, the interior lights shine brightly, showing no one is in there. "This is me. Thanks. Bye."

I sigh. A person can only apologize so many times. If the person on the receiving end isn't ready to hear it, there's not much to be done—a hard truth I'm coming to realize. "I'll wait until you're in your car."

She rolls her eyes, then opens the back door and tosses her bag onto the back seat. She doesn't even glance my way when she gets into the front seat and starts the car.

I knock on the car window, pushing my luck. Her hands are

tightly gripping the steering wheel. She sighs, and for the first time, I wonder if keeping the wall between us is a real effort for her. After a pause, she reluctantly rolls down the window.

She doesn't bother turning in my direction, instead looking straight ahead.

Here goes nothing. My last-ditch effort.

"Shayna, I know I've been pestering you about forgiving me and it's clear that you have no intention of doing so and I guess as much as I hate it, that's fair. I hurt you, and I really am sorry. I should've told you right away about the bet so that we could've moved forward and put it behind us—if that would've even been possible. Maybe things would've been different. But I'm not trying to make your life miserable again, so I'll back off. I hope at some point we can become friends or, at the bare minimum, friendly colleagues. Regardless, I'll stop putting pressure on you to forgive me. I did what I did, and I have to live with the consequences. But please know that I do regret hurting you and screwing up a good thing between us. If you do ever want to talk about it, even if it's just to cuss me out, you know where to find me." I tap the roof of her car and turn and walk away toward my SUV, feeling unsettled.

I haven't felt this down since the Kingsmen didn't make it to the playoffs last year. I guess you reap what you sow.

ten

. . .

Shayna

Maybe things would have been different.

Lee's words have run on repeat through my head for the past two weeks since I ran into him at the gym, and I hate it. I kick myself for giving any kind of mental space to what might've been between Lee Burrows and me.

When I accepted the position with Kingsmen, I knew working with him every day would be a challenge, but I honestly thought that our interactions would be minimal and we could pretend the past didn't exist. I had no idea he'd even care or remember me.

So far, that plan has been blown to smithereens because Lee definitely still affects me. Not only does he remember me, but he's also dying for my forgiveness.

He's a man of his word though, because he pretty much steers clear of me. When we do have to interact, he keeps things cool and professional. I wish I could say that makes me happy, but the truth is that I'm more agitated than ever toward him. Which brings up the question, what do I want? Because I'm not happy with either option.

Was I just enjoying his attention before and I couldn't admit it to myself? Purposely being bitchy about something that happened eight years ago? And if so, what does that say about me?

Now that training camp is over and the team's roster is complete, to celebrate, as well as raise money for a local charity, there's a gala this evening. Everyone from the Kingsmen is invited, as well as members of the press, and even though I should probably be excited, I'm dreading it because all the attention will be on Lee. I'll have to watch everyone fawn over him all night, proclaiming what an amazing guy he is.

Plus, I know he's probably going to look hot as hell in a tuxedo and have women surrounding him all night. Which will only agitate me even more.

My Uber driver pulls up in front of Bryce's place. I text Bryce to let her know we're here, and she appears a minute later. Every member of the team is allowed to have a plus-one with them tonight, and Bryce is mine, even though she could attend anyway with her press credentials.

She slides into the back seat beside me. "Love the hair."

I finger the pearl-covered clip holding my hair back on one side of my head. The rest of my hair is set in waves so it reaches just below my shoulders.

I've really grown to like Bryce in the few weeks we've known each other. It doesn't hurt that she can help a girl feel confident when she's unsure. Tonight is my first social event with the team. I'm confident when I'm at work, assessing a player and putting a plan together for their treatment, but not so much when I'm hobnobbing with the players, their significant others, and the team executives.

I may not be the same shy, introverted girl anymore, but I'm out of my element with these types of things. Bryce, on the other hand, thrives in the type of environment we're heading into tonight, so I'm happy to have her by my side.

We reach the hotel, exit the Uber, and make our way inside. The hotel is beautiful and reminiscent of the Gilded Age with its beautiful carved moldings and exquisite chandeliers. Bryce leads us toward the ballroom—she's been to this event for a few years in a row since she started with the *Chronicle*.

We stop at the coat check just outside the ballroom, and we each hand over our coats and take our tickets from the attendant.

"Wow. You look smoking." Bryce eyes me from head to toe.

I smooth my palm over the red fabric of my dress with the hand not holding my black clutch. "Are you sure? I'm second-guessing going for such a bold color."

I chose a deep-red floor-length dress that swoops down in the front and has a sort of half cape that skims over my shoulders and hangs behind my arms and back. I thought it was elegant when I tried it on, but now I'm second-guessing the cleavage for a work event.

"Do not second-guess that dress. It's gorgeous and so are you."

Leaning into her, I say in a low voice, "I'm not showing too much boob?"

"Tits are always in, my friend." She laughs. "Seriously though, your dress is stunning. You have nothing to worry about. Just look around at the amount of boobs getting air time in this place."

I scan our immediate area and see that she's right. All kinds of women are showing more cleavage than me, and they look classy and elegant. I'm not going to stand out any more than them.

"Okay." I let out a rush of air. "You look amazing too, by the way. In case I didn't say that already."

"Thanks. The minute I tried this dress on, I knew I had to have it."

I envy Bryce's effortless confidence and ability to take a compliment. But she's right—her cream dress looks amazing on her olive skin.

"Want to get a drink?" I suggest, needing a glass of wine to help ease my nerves.

"Sure. Tell me, are you nervous because this is your first big work function or does it have to do with a certain quarterback?"

My head whips in her direction. "I told you, he's left me alone ever since his speech in the parking lot." I smile at people I don't recognize as we walk through the crowd.

She turns to look at me as she pushes past a group of older men chatting in a small circle. "Okay, so it's just the work thing and worrying about making a good impression then?"

"Mostly."

She raises her perfectly arched eyebrows.

"A little of both, I guess."

We reach the bar and stand in the small line to wait our turn.

"If he approaches you tonight, do you want me to save you?" she asks.

I nod. "Absolutely. The less time I'm able to spend around him, the better. Do you want me to do the same if I see you with Miles or Brady?"

She barks out a laugh and waves me off. "Please, I can handle myself."

I chuckle. I have no doubt she's right.

Once I have red wine in hand, we turn and face the room. A few players mill around. Some of them appear to have dates, and others are chatting with other players. My heart skips a beat when my eyes land on Lee because yeah, I was right. He's a whole other level wearing a tuxedo.

His hair is more slicked back than usual, and his face is completely clean-shaven. Normally he has an effortless, unkempt look that suits his personality. But tonight, he's all sophistication and class, and he pulls it off just as well.

My stomach sours when I see who he's talking to. I don't recognize the woman, but she's beautiful—petite with long dark curls that hang down her back and bright, expressive eyes. The two of them are laughing at something she just said, and the sight of Lee enjoying himself with another woman twists my stomach in knots.

"How about we go check out the seating plan and find our table?" Bryce suggests, obviously seeing what I am and tearing me away.

"Yes. Let's." I drag my gaze away from Lee and who I presume is his date and follow Bryce to the far side of the ballroom.

Why didn't it dawn on me that he'd have a plus-one too? Of course he'd have a date. He has his pick of women and I actually assumed he'd show up alone? I'm an idiot.

But the better question is, why do I care?

When we reach the board, I breathe a sigh of relief that we've been seated with a couple of the other athletic trainers. At least I won't have to struggle to keep my dinner down while watching Lee's date fawn all over him.

"Well… at least we're not at his table," Bryce says.

"What do you mean?" I don't know why I bother to play dumb. We may not have known each other for a long time, but Bryce always seems to be able to tell what I'm thinking but not saying.

"Please, you were practically eye-stabbing that woman Lee was laughing with."

I arch an eyebrow. "Eye-stabbing?"

She shrugs. "Sure, like eye-fucking, but the opposite."

"The opposite of fucking is stabbing?"

She waves me off. "You know what I mean and don't bother to deny it."

I don't. There's no point. "Let's go figure out where table number thirty-four is."

She doesn't argue, letting the subject drop. We wind through the tables until we find ours. Nobody else is there yet. They're mingling since it's cocktail hour.

I heave a sigh because I should be doing the same. If I want to make a place for myself on this team, I need to get to know the people I work with better in a social setting.

After I set my clutch on the table, I sip my wine. "I should go mingle."

"Same." Bryce sets her purse down beside mine.

"I'll meet you back here before dinner is served."

She nods and heads off into the crowd, no doubt looking for her new story.

I turn in the opposite direction with drink in hand, heading toward where Brady is talking with Chase and Darius. Brady is all personality and we get along well. Maybe it's because we're both newcomers to the team, but I suspect it's more that Brady is all charm and gets along with anyone. I don't know Chase well, but he seems like a man of few words —most of the words I've heard him speak have been profanities. Darius is one of the Kingsmen's defensive ends and I've only ever seen him upbeat and joking around. This group seems like a safe bet before I find either of my bosses to say hello.

"Here comes trouble," Brady says, sliding his arm around my back and kissing my cheek.

"That feels a lot like the pot calling the kettle black," I say.

He grins, but doesn't deny it.

"You clean up well," Darius says, waggling his eyebrows. "I'm probably not supposed to say that, but hopefully you don't mind me saying."

Chase rolls his eyes and concentrates on something over Darius's shoulder.

I smile. "I don't know about any other woman, but speaking for myself, I don't mind your compliment at all. If you knew how much time, money, and work went into the hair, makeup, and dress, you'd understand why I'll gladly accept your compliments tonight."

All three guys laugh. Well, Brady and Darius laugh. Chase

does this thing that sounds more like a grunt but might be his version of a laugh.

"You ready for a good season?" Brady asks. It's easy to see the competitive gleam in his eyes when he talks about football. "We were just saying how we think we stand a real chance with the team the Kingsmen have put together this year."

He's not wrong, but I can't help but play around a bit anyway. "Don't you guys think you're going to win every year?"

Chase shrugs. "What else are we gonna think?"

"Gotta go into it thinking you're the best," Darius adds.

"Even if you know deep down, you're not," Brady says.

They all laugh, obviously having been in that situation before. I won't ask if it was with the Kingsmen.

"The team is going to do amazing this year, I have no doubt." I smile, bringing my wineglass to my mouth, and sip at the same time someone behind accidentally bumps me. A small amount of wine dribbles from my lip and drips down. "Shit."

I wipe the wine dribbling down my chin with the back of my hand and look down at my dress. I don't see anything, but then again, the wine is almost the same color as the fabric.

"At least it won't show up on your dress." I stiffen at the sound of Lee's voice. He's standing next to me and his vision is zeroed in on my cleavage.

"Excuse me, guys. I'm going to head to the restroom and see if I can get rid of this spot on my dress." Never mind the fact that I don't actually see a spot. I need to escape his nearness because my feelings are all over the place now with Lee standing beside me and that's the last thing I can handle.

Without waiting for any of them to answer, I spin on my heel and walk away.

eleven

. . .

Lee

"What gives with you two, Burrows?" Darius asks, nodding in Shayna's direction.

"There's a story there?" Chase adds.

I tip back my drink. "I don't know what you're talking about."

"Every time I see you two within five yards of each other, there's friction." Darius hits me on the shoulder, and I just barely suppress my cringe.

My shoulder's been a little tender lately. Nothing big, but enough that I've noticed.

"Maybe she just gets tongue-tied because I'm the QB1." I flash a wide smile and tip my drink back to avoid having to answer any other questions.

The guys let it slide when Dr. Frampton comes by to say hello. We chat with him for a minute before we're told to make our way to our seats for the dinner portion of the evening.

Usually I don't mind these things. It's a good chance to get to know some of the guys on the team better and build a bond with them outside of the field. But ever since Shayna entered the room, I've felt agitated.

She was gorgeous tonight, which isn't surprising. Every man here has noticed, giving her second glances, their eyes roaming up and down her body. It's impossible not to with that dress she's wearing—classy and sophisticated, yet sexy as fuck. That's Shayna in a nutshell, and after tonight, everyone will know it and she'll have guys sniffing around for sure. It's why I wish she would have shown up on my arm tonight.

The entire dinner is spent with me pretending to listen to the other people at my table and joining in on the conversation, but I keep sneaking glances at Shayna because I have a perfect view of her table. I can't see her face, but I can see the back of her head, and there's a whole helluva lot you can read from body language alone.

For instance, she prefers talking to the man on her right, who must be the date of the other athletic trainer to his right, and she's trying her best to avoid conversation with the guy directly across the table from her. Also, it's clear that she and Bryce are tight now—they've been chatting and giggling and whispering the entire dinner.

"Burrows, you paying attention?" Miles pulls me back to where my focus should be.

I put down my fork. "Sorry, what'd I miss?"

"Twyla has something to tell us all." Miles motions to his little sister with a proud smile.

Most of the guys know Twyla pretty well. She's kind of like all our little sisters. She visits so often from where she lives on the East Coast that we've all grown to feel protective of her. Maybe me more than others since I've known her for longer.

Her hands are in her lap, and she draws in a deep breath as though maybe she's nervous about whatever she has to say. "Last week, Mathew proposed, and I accepted. I'm getting married!" She holds up her left hand and a large diamond sparkles on her ring finger.

The entire table breaks out in applause and congratulations. Everyone slides out of their chairs to give her a hug and congratulations. Miles's eyes are wide and his mouth hangs open. I smack him on the back as I push my chair back and stand, walking over to Twyla to give her a hug and my congratulations.

I'm sure she decided to announce it here in front of everyone at the table because Miles is like a big brother pit bull and he especially doesn't like Twyla's boyfriend, now fiancé, Mathew. But Miles's opinion matters a lot to her, so I'm sure she's nervous to see what he thinks of her upcoming nuptials. If he's smart, he'll pretend he's excited for her, no matter how he really feels.

When I back up from Twyla, Miles hugs his sister and wishes her congratulations. Twyla's eyes are filled with relief.

We all toast to Twyla, then I excuse myself to use the restroom. When I leave the men's room, Shayna is making her way down the hall toward the ladies' room. I call her name. Why, I have no idea. She's made it clear she wants me to leave her alone, and if I didn't already know that, the scowl she gave me in front of the guys earlier would make it clear.

She doesn't slow, so I jog to catch up with her.

"What's the rush?" I ask.

"I want to get back to my table." She stops but doesn't turn her head to look at me, so I come around her to stand in front of her.

"Did I say something earlier to piss you off? I wasn't the one who bumped you."

She sighs. "I realize that, Lee. Not everything is about you."

My forehead wrinkles. "Are you all right?"

"Shouldn't you get back to your table? I'm sure your date won't be happy if she finds you in the hallway talking to me." She crosses her arms, and I pretend not to notice the way her cleavage goes from a ten to a twelve. I must look as confused as I feel because she says, "What, you don't think she'll care? Maybe not. Then again, I've never known you to be the smartest guy when it comes to women."

I shake my head. "I came alone."

She guffaws and rolls her eyes. "I saw you with her earlier, and don't go getting a big ego, no, I wasn't looking for you in the crowd, I just happened to notice."

I stare at her for a beat, and her arms drop to her sides. I've never seen this side of Shayna.

"Seriously?" She shakes her head, as though I'm so predictable or something. "It was obvious the way you two were with each other."

I raise my hands. "I swear I don't know what you're talking about."

"Long curly hair, green dress, beautiful woman… any of this ring a bell?"

It's then I realize she's talking about Twyla, and a slow smile spreads across my face. Her eyes narrow more and she inhales deeply. If she's this worked up about me chatting with my best friend's sister, it must mean she cares on some level. I can't strip the smile off my face because I'm so damn happy.

"Ah… you're jealous?" I arch an eyebrow.

She scoffs. "In your dreams. I'm just thinking about the poor girl sitting there in the ballroom waiting for you to return while you're out here chatting me up."

"Sure you are."

"It's true." She raises her chin in a prideful way.

I step closer to her and lean in, whispering in her ear, "For the record, if I saw you here with a date tonight and I saw him looking at you the way *I've* been looking at you all night, I'd want to send my fist through his face. Right or wrong, I'd be jealous, so don't feel bad about it. And just so it's abundantly clear, that's Miles's sister, Twyla. She's in town visiting, so he invited her along. If you saw us laughing together, it was likely at his expense. And yes, she's beautiful, but I never have, and I never would, think of doing the things to her that I want so desperately to do to you."

I walk away, leaving Shayna standing there with flushed cheeks and apparently unsure of what to say. Which is appropriate. Even I don't know where we go now that I've laid my entire hand out there.

twelve

. . .

Shayna

After I use the facilities, I stumble back to the table in a daze, Lee's words echoing through my head like a constant reverberation causing an ache between my legs.

The way I've been looking at you all night…

I'd be jealous…

I want so desperately to do to you…

Every part of me wishes I was appalled or insulted by his forwardness, but my body betrays me. The area between my thighs hums, and my nipples are tight under the fabric of my dress. That man still gets under my skin and in my head.

"What happened in the bathroom? You're all flushed," Bryce says when I sit at the table.

"I'll tell you later," I murmur, reaching for my wineglass and finishing what's left.

Bryce looks over her shoulder, presumably at the table Lee is seated at, then gives me a knowing look. "Can't wait to hear all about it."

I do my best throughout the rest of dinner to engage with my fellow tablemates, but Lee's gaze on my back feels like a brand. Maybe it's my imagination. Maybe it's wishful thinking.

If I'm really honest with myself, I can admit that once Lee vowed to leave me alone and not press me for forgiveness, I missed his attention.

Jesus, the man has my head spinning. There's no way I can continue like this much longer. I need some kind of resolution.

When dinner wraps up, Bryce goes off to mingle and I decide to head to the other side of the room to check out the silent auction items. I have no plans—or budget—to bid on anything, but I'm curious what's up for grabs.

Helicopter tour of the city… a week in Turks and Caicos… tickets to the Grammys. I knew the people in the room were wealthy, but holy shit are they connected.

I stop at a week aboard a superyacht. I've never even been on a cruise, and to be honest, I'm not sure I'd want to be stuck on the high seas with thousands of people, but a private yacht is different altogether.

Studying the pictures of the ship, I allow myself a moment to imagine what it would be like to be afforded such luxury. Growing up, we couldn't afford extravagant family vacations, and the handful we did take were always shorter road trips.

I eye the picture of the chaise lounges on the sundeck and I close my eyes, imagining the sun warming my skin and inhaling the salty air.

"Shayna, do you have a moment? I wanted to introduce you to someone."

My eyes snap open and I turn to Dr. Carlisle standing at my side with a man who needs no introduction because I know who he is—heck, he's the reason we're all here.

Giles Hanover owns the San Francisco Kingsmen.

"Hi, Dr. Carlisle." I smile at them both.

"I keep telling you to call me Jerry." Then he turns his attention to Mr. Hanover. "Shayna Kudrow, this is Giles Hanover, owner of the San Francisco Kingsmen. Shayna is our newest addition to the medical team."

Mr. Hanover holds his hand out to me.

I set my clutch on the auction table since I have a glass of wine in my other hand and shake his hand. "Pleasure to meet you, Mr. Hanover."

"Welcome to the team. I trust you're enjoying your time with us thus far?" His voice is deep and somehow suits his tall and intimidating persona.

"I am. Everyone has been very welcoming."

He gives a sharp nod. "Glad to hear it. We would have crossed paths sooner, but my wife's mother passed away, so we've been in Europe taking care of all the arrangements."

"I'm sorry for your loss," I say.

He waves away my concern. "The old bat had it coming. She was in her nineties and hated everyone and everything. I think it was pure spite that kept her alive this long."

Not knowing what to say to that, I give him a wan smile.

"Well, I think you'll be pleased when you see the guys on the field for the first time this year. We've got a good group to work with."

Mr. Hanover clamps his meaty hand on Dr. Carlisle's shoulder. "As long as Burrow's arm remains in top form, we're bound to make the playoffs, right, Shayna?" He winks.

I smile, though I'm not sure how genuine it looks since his mentioning Lee has thrown me off. Lee is his star player and commands the largest salary of anyone on the team. Of course his hopes for a great season are riding on him.

"That's right. The Kingsmen have a real shot this year, no doubt."

Mr. Hanover nods as though he's happy I've agreed with him. "Tell me, are you a fan of football, Shayna, or did you accept this job because you wanted to be an athletic trainer?"

"My dad made sure I was a football fan, but I must admit that I grew up a Green Bay fan." I cringe and both men laugh.

"We won't hold it against you," Mr. Hanover says.

We chat for a few more minutes about some of the more

memorable plays in the league from last season before both men get pulled away by someone else.

My hand dips to my stomach as we say goodbye.

It's okay, you did all right. I had to meet the team's owner at some point, but that was nerve-wracking nonetheless.

I head back to my table, and since Bryce isn't there, I chat with a couple of the wives of my coworkers. Apparently, the guys are off at the bar getting another drink.

At some point I spot Bryce in the crowd. I stand to join her, but the crowd parts and she's talking to Miles and neither of them looks too pleased. On second thought, I'll stay here. I have enough of my own drama I'm trying to avoid tonight. I don't need to get sucked into anyone else's.

Deciding that I have to force myself to socialize and not sit here at the table all night, I top off my wineglass with the bottle from dinner and walk around the perimeter of the ballroom. Guests are dancing and mingling around the tables. I don't see anyone I know, but when I stop to observe the people on the dance floor for a minute, an older woman in her eighties approaches me and strikes up a conversation.

Turns out the very nice woman is Giles Hanover's mother, and I get stuck talking to her forever. When she insists on introducing me to her husband and their friends at her table, practically forcing me to take a seat with them, forever feels like it turns into infinity.

By the time I manage to extricate myself, at least half of the guests have already departed.

Shit. I'd better find Bryce.

I head to our table but don't find her there, so I check the couples slow dancing on the dance floor. She's not there either.

Maybe I'll text her to see where she's at and if she's ready to leave.

I set my wineglass on our table and reach for my purse where it was most of dinner. My stomach slides to the floor when I realize my purse isn't there. The sick feeling spreads through my abdomen and my eyes widen.

Where the hell is my purse? I lift the tablecloth, searching under the table and all the chairs. Nothing.

My mind frantically runs through everywhere I've been tonight. I remember I had my clutch with me when I was perusing the auction items. I leave my wineglass on the table and rush back over to the auction item tables, only to find they've all been packed up and my purse isn't anywhere.

Damn it.

I swing around and scan the room again in search of Bryce. She's nowhere to be found.

She's not the type of person to leave without telling me. Maybe she tried to get a hold of me and because I didn't have my purse with my phone in it, I didn't know. I'm supposed to crash at her place tonight and she was going to drive me back to Santa Clara tomorrow.

First things first, I need to find my purse. I do a quick sweep of the room, looking on all the tables to see if my purse somehow ended up on one of them. When I don't find it, I decide to do a more thorough check while also looking at the purses the guests are holding. Perhaps someone picked mine up by accident thinking it was theirs?

Another trip around the room doesn't turn up anything, and now there're even fewer people here and it's clear to me that Bryce isn't in this ballroom.

"What's wrong?" Lee stands off to the side, a concerned look on his face. The bow tie of his tuxedo is undone and hangs loose around his collar. That, coupled with the first two buttons of his shirt being undone, makes him look next-level sexy.

"Nothing. I'm handling it." I walk away, but he stops me with his hand on my upper arm.

"I've watched you circle this ballroom twice. You're practically in tears. Tell me what's wrong."

I yank my arm away. "I don't need your help. I said I'm handling it."

"I know you probably *can* handle it, but I'm here offering to help, so why not just take me up on it?"

He's right. I know he is. The only reason I'm so openly hostile toward him at this point is my ever-present lust for the man.

I'm not good at letting other people help me, but in this case, I really could use a hand.

"I lost my purse. I think I left it on one of the auction tables, but it's not there anymore."

His lips press into a thin line. "All right, what's it look like?" I describe it to him, and he nods. "I'll figure out who cleaned up the auction tables and see if they saw it. You keep looking in here. Check under the tables too, in case it fell off and got pushed under the tablecloth somehow."

He doesn't wait for me to answer before taking off in the direction of the empty auction tables.

Though I'm not used to letting someone help me, I find myself reluctantly grateful Lee stepped in.

thirteen

. . .

Lee

"No luck on my end. How about you?" I push a hand through my hair, annoyed that I can't be some white knight and deliver Shayna her missing purse.

She pinches the bridge of her nose. "Nothing."

"I spoke to one of the hotel staff and they said one of the people from the charity packed up all the auction stuff. She was going to get me a name and number, but it'll probably be tomorrow by the time it's figured out." I gently pull Shayna's hand away from her face.

Her big aqua eyes meet mine, sparkling with unshed tears.

"Hey, it's not that bad." God, I want to pull her into my chest, but she'd probably castrate me.

"It is that bad. Everything is in there! My phone, my money, my bank card, the keys to my apartment. Thank god I didn't throw my credit cards in there. I have no idea where Bryce is and I'm supposed to stay with her tonight. Now I have no way of getting back to Santa Clara."

I take her hand and lead her toward the exit. "All hope is not lost. Let's check with the hotel staff to see if they have a lost and found. Maybe someone found it and turned it in."

She nods and allows me to lead her by the hand. The ballroom is mostly empty at this point, and the staff is taking the table linens off the tables and breaking down the room.

A quick visit to the front desk of the hotel doesn't turn up Shayna's purse, and she looks more dejected than ever.

"Do you have any rooms available?" I ask the clerk after she's checked—twice at my behest—for the purse.

Shayna's head whips in my direction and she scowls. "No."

"For you, not us. You said you had nowhere to stay."

The woman behind the desk cringes. "It wouldn't matter anyway, Mr. Burrows. We're all booked."

"I couldn't afford it anyway," Shayna mumbles.

I thank the receptionist and lead Shayna away.

"I'd cover the room," I say in a low voice.

That only seems to piss her off more. "No way. I do not need you to pay for my room. I'd just have to pay you back, and after what I paid for this dress, these shoes, and my glam tonight, I can't afford the extra expense. Hence why Bryce was going to drop me at home tomorrow, rather than me taking an Uber home tonight."

I can't blame her. An Uber all the way from the city to Santa Clara on a Saturday night would cost a small fortune. I can easily afford it now, but my life wasn't always like this and the last thing I want to do is to make Shayna feel insecure about her financial position.

"Okay, well… let's call Bryce on my phone and see if she answers. I can always drive you to her."

Shayna cringes.

"What?"

"I don't know her number."

I look at her in disbelief.

"What? Who remembers anyone's number these days? They add their contact to your phone and you press the screen where their name is."

I don't bother telling her that I could recite her college phone number without a problem. There were so many nights over the years when I typed it out only to delete it. "So what then? Do you want me to drive you over to her place and see if she's there?"

She looks at me hesitantly for a beat. "Sure, I'd appreciate that."

"Let me grab my coat from the coat check."

Her head drops forward with a groan.

"What?"

"I can't even get my jacket because I don't have my coat check ticket."

"C'mon. I'll make sure you get your coat."

We head back toward the ballroom, and I hand the attendant my ticket. "My friend here lost her purse, and her coat check ticket was inside. Is there any possibility she could go back there and find her coat?"

The teenager working the coat check glances around. "I'm sorry, sir, but I can't do that. I could lose my job and my manager already wants to fire me because last week a couple snuck in because I was in crisis with my best friend and on the phone and… it ended up being the groom and a bridesmaid that snuck in… and then the bride's dad found them… and a big fight started and—"

I hold out my hand to stop the poor girl from telling me her life story. I hate to do this, but at the same time, I hope to impress Shayna a little with my next move. "Are you sure? You'd really be helping us out. I could get you tickets to a game. Do you enjoy—"

I stop speaking when Shayna's hand lands on my forearm. She's not touching my skin, but she might as well be. I swear I can feel the heat of her hand through my tuxedo jacket and dress shirt.

"It's fine," she says to the girl, whose shoulders relax. "You can just get his jacket."

I turn to face her. "What are you doing?"

"That poor girl was obviously freaking out and didn't know what to do once you started pressuring her. My jacket is the least of my worries. I'll figure it out tomorrow."

When the girl returns, I fish a twenty out of my wallet and hand it to her.

"Thanks so much." Her smile is wide now.

"Don't mention it." I lead Shayna toward the front of the hotel and pause before we head through the revolving doors. "Here." I wrap my jacket over her shoulders.

"You don't have to give me yours." She tries to slide the jacket off, but I stop her.

"It's just a jacket, Shayna. Relax." I head outside and hand the valet my ticket, then return to join her inside.

We don't say a word while we wait for the attendant to return with my SUV. He does, and we head outside. Shayna looks hesitant about getting inside when the guy opens the door for her, but she does.

I try not to think about how good it feels to have her beside me in my vehicle as though we're a real couple. As if I'm driving us home and when we get there, I'll slide down the zipper of her dress, slowly peeling the red dress off her naked body. How my bulge will be evident and her hand will unbuckle and unzip me, freeing my hard-on. I'd lay her out on my bed…

"LEE!" Shayna pulls me back from my imagination. Damn, it was just getting good.

I shake my head. "Where does Bryce live?" She gives me the address, and I input it into the vehicle's GPS while we wait at a red light. "I used to rent a place a few blocks away from there when I moved to the city."

"Where do you live now?" She hasn't looked at me once since we've gotten in the car, but I take it as a good sign that she's choosing to engage in conversation with me.

"I'm in a condo over in the Russian Hill area."

She chuckles, and it's as if someone plugged my heart into an electric socket because I haven't heard her laugh since before everything went to shit in college.

"I'm not sure why I even asked. I don't know many places in the city yet."

I smile and flick my signal on to make a right. "It's down near the water, close to the marina."

She nods. "Ah, where the rich people live."

I look at her a little sheepishly.

"Oh jeez, don't feel bad about it, Lee. You've worked hard to get where you are."

She's not wrong. I have worked my ass off to be one of the best quarterbacks in the league. I work harder and longer, study more tape, and make sure I'm in peak physical condition. Still, when someone points out my wealth, especially someone who's not in the same financial position as I am, I always feel a little uncomfortable. Maybe because I know what it's like to be poor.

"We're almost there," I say to change the subject. "I'll park and go up to the door with you."

She gives me a look that says I'm being ridiculous. It reminds me a lot of the look she'd give me when she tutored me in college and I attempted to flirt with her. "You'll never find a parking spot close to the building. I'll run up to the door and buzz her."

I frown. Unfortunately, she's not wrong. I glance at the heels she's wearing. There's no way those are comfortable to walk in after she's worn them all night. Especially in San Francisco with all the hills.

"Fine. I'll double-park right out front so I can see you."

She nods, and I park in front of Bryce's building next to a car. "Be right back, hopefully to tell you she's home."

Shayna exits, rounds the front of my SUV, and goes inside the small lobby. She presses a button on the wall and looks inside. She presses it again and waits some more. Her fingers are now in her mouth and she glances back at me, then stares inside one more time. No one is coming.

From the way she's walking toward the car with a frown, it's clear Bryce isn't home. She opens the door and plops herself down in the seat.

"No go?"

She shakes her head. "I have no idea where she could be. Now I'm kind of worried."

"I'm sure she's fine. Maybe she saw someone she knew at the gala and went out with them after. Or maybe she's hooking up with someone?"

"Maybe…" She doesn't sound convinced.

"So… what now?"

She turns her head and looks at me, worrying her bottom lip.

"I can drive you home—"

"My keys are in my purse, and since I don't have my phone, I don't even have the landlord's number to call him. I barely know my neighbors, and I can't fathom waking one of them up in the middle of the night to get it. Ugh!" Her head drops back against the seat and she stares up through my sunroof. "This is so frustrating."

I could voice the idea I had earlier, but will she think I'm being an opportunistic douchebag? But it's clear Shayna can't get into her apartment even if she can get home and she won't let me pay for a hotel room for her, so really, what are her options?

"Can I make a suggestion without you getting upset?"

She blows out a breath and turns to face me.

"You could spend the night at my place." When her expression turns into a scowl, I hold up my hands. "You'd stay in the guest room. I'm not suggesting this to try to get you into my bed or anything. Believe me, you've made it abundantly clear you don't want to be there." I pinch the bridge of my nose. "What I mean is that you could stay there, and then in the morning we can sort out your purse, where Bryce might be, and how to get you into your apartment if we can't locate your purse in the light of day."

She bites her bottom lip, staring at me.

I sigh. "I swear I'm just trying to help you. Nothing more."

Shayna doesn't respond for a beat. "It wouldn't mean anything if I stayed over."

"I know."

"It doesn't change anything."

I nod. "I know that too."

"All right." She leans back in her seat and crosses her arms.

I get the sense that she's sulking. That's okay though. We've made progress tonight and I'll take what I can get— even if she's giving in reluctantly.

fourteen

· · ·

Shayna

On the elevator up to Lee's condo, I act as if it's no big deal that I'm going to spend the night at his place, but the truth is I'm freaking out.

Tonight is the most interaction I've had with him since I arrived in San Francisco, and the fact is, we'll be alone all night in his condo. Even if everything has been completely platonic tonight, it's hard not to let my mind wander. What if he was just taking me home? What if we had been on a date? Memories of our times together in college distract me until the elevator dings.

I startle as the doors slide open right into Lee's condo. The decor is exactly what I expected from a single guy, but homier. When I follow him into the large living area, it's not stark and void of life. You can tell someone really lives here.

There are photos of friends and family on the built-in entertainment center, and a few *Sports Illustrated* magazines litter the coffee table beside a half-drunk cup of coffee. One seat cushion is more indented than the rest, revealing he has a certain spot he always sits in to watch television.

Through the wall-to-wall windows, the city lights sparkle

below, and the Golden Gate Bridge is lit up in the distance. His view alone says he paid a lot for this place.

"It's really nice." My speech is stilted because I feel so awkward being here.

Lee looks just as uncomfortable, his hands shoved into his tuxedo pants as he rocks back on his heels. "Can I get you anything? You hungry? Thirsty?"

I shake my head. "No, I'm good. Just…" I glance at my dress and inwardly scream. "Can I borrow something to sleep in?"

A strangled noise slips out, but he quickly clears his throat. "Of course. Sure. Yeah. I'll show you the guest room, then I'll grab you something."

I follow him through the kitchen and dining area, past an office, and down a hallway. He walks into a room with a large bed covered in a cream comforter. The walnut headboard and furniture give off a natural and cozy feeling.

I step into the room as he asks, "Will this work?"

I chuckle. "Yeah. Barely."

He laughs and runs his hand through his hair. "I'll go get you something to change into."

He disappears from the doorway. The condo is so quiet, I hear him heading farther down the hall to what I assume must be his bedroom.

I plop down on the bed, testing its firmness. I wonder if anyone has ever even slept on this mattress. It's like brand new. Lee appears in the doorway, so I jolt up off the mattress.

"Here you go." He offers me a pile of folded-up clothes. "They're gonna be big, but hopefully you can manage them. If not, just let me know."

I nod and accept the clothes. "Great. Thanks."

He stares at me then nods. "Okay, well… I'll leave you to it. You should find a spare toothbrush in one of the drawers in the en suite bathroom, along with some toothpaste. Feel free to have a shower if you like too."

I get an image of him in the shower down the hall from me. He's probably got one with exposed glass all around and five different showerheads. How I wouldn't mind showering with him.

No, bad Shayna.

I have to remember he's a liar and brought me nothing but misery eight years ago. I cannot depend on him to do the right thing.

Although letting me stay here tonight was a really nice thing for him to do. Ever since I came to San Francisco, I've given him the cold shoulder and not allowed him to properly apologize for his actions all those years ago. And here he's helped me all night after I lost my purse, eventually bringing me home to his condo and something to wear.

I look up from the pile of clothes. "Thank you, Lee. Thanks for everything tonight."

His tongue slides out and licks his lips. There's so much awkward tension in the room, I'm at a loss for what to do.

"Don't mention it," he murmurs and walks toward the door, closing it behind him.

A large rush of air leaves my lungs once I'm by myself.

I'm slipping. As I go into the bathroom, I realize I've been keeping him at arm's length because deep down, Lee might just be the guy I fell in love with in college. He might be that good guy who did a very stupid thing. But how do I ever trust him with my heart again?

———

I awaken with a start and glance around the dark room. It takes me a moment to remember I'm at Lee's.

Sitting in bed, I moisten my lips. Wine always dehydrates me.

My throat is so dry it hurts, and I'll never be able to fall back asleep unless I drink some water. I climb out of bed and tiptoe to the door, arms outstretched in the dark so I don't bump into anything.

I fumble for the door handle, and I'm relieved to find the hallway is lit with low lighting so I can see where I'm going. I walk down the hallway toward the kitchen and quietly open cabinets, searching for a glass.

After finding one, I step over to the sink and turn on the faucet, waiting until it's cool to fill the glass. Once it's filled, I turn around and see a man.

"Sorry," his deep, groggy voice says.

It's too late. The cold glass slips from my grasp, but Lee bolts forward, bending to catch it before it shatters on the floor. Cold water splashes out of the cup and against my leg.

"Wow. Good reflexes." My hand presses against my hammering heart.

He straightens to his full height. "Sorry, didn't mean to startle you."

He leans past me to set the glass on the counter and my tongue ties at him shirtless with a pair of loose-fitting navy pajama pants hanging low on his hips. His abs on display and the defined *V* that leads down past the waistband of his pants cause my mouth to become drier.

"Hold still," he softly says.

I hold my breath, unsure of what he's about to do. Of what I *want* him to do.

He's so close, his breath tickles my neck as he leans in again, reaching past me for… a… dish towel.

I should not be disappointed.

Lee bends and runs the towel up my calf where the water splashed. "Hang on." After he dries my legs, he uses the dish towel on the floor. "I don't want you to slip."

He looks up, kneeling in front of me, and my teeth press down on my bottom lip when our eyes lock. His gaze flicks to his oversized T-shirt I knotted in front, and I'm aware my nipples must be poking out, then back up to meet my eyes again. The ache is unnerving.

The featherlight tip of his finger runs from behind my knee down to my ankle. When he's done, he stands and tosses the towel on the counter behind me and steps back.

The disappointment flaring in my chest pisses me off. There is no way that I'm upset he didn't try to kiss me, is there?

This duality going on inside me is driving me crazy. I mean, I definitely was pissed when I first started on with the team, but after his speech that night at the gym, I felt myself waning. And after tonight, I'm remembering what drew me to him in the first place.

If I want to keep my heart safe, the best path forward is to continue to hate him and keep him at arm's distance, but that's proving difficult. Maybe it's better to put the past behind us and move forward as friends. Then I can get resolution and a sense of where my feelings are for him.

I glance up from the floor and Lee's looking at me with wide eyes, his hip resting on the counter and his arms crossed over that mouthwatering chest of his.

"What?" My forehead wrinkles.

"Nothing."

"You're looking at me weird."

He sighs and pushes his hand through his hair, which makes his waves poofy. Another great look on him. This fresh-out-of-bed, messy-hair thing really works for him, just as well as the tuxedo one.

"You'll get mad if I say it."

Now I'm really intrigued. I raise an eyebrow.

"It's just that… you're sexy as fuck in my clothes."

Heat flares in my body. My cheeks, my breasts, between my legs. "Oh… thanks."

He frowns. "Anyway, I just came in to grab a drink too. There's water in the fridge if you prefer filtered." Lee walks over to the fridge and pulls out a bottle of water, gesturing toward me with it.

I nod and he slides it down the island counter. "Thanks."

"No problem." He turns to leave the kitchen.

For some reason, I don't want him to leave. All this unsettled business between us is brimming inside me. If we don't talk tonight, I'm not going to get any sleep.

"Lee, wait."

He stops with his back to me but doesn't turn around.

"I think… I think you were right."

"About what?" He keeps his back to me. All his muscles look tense, as though he's worried about what I'm going to say.

"We should try to move forward."

He whips around, his eyebrows high and his mouth open. "For real?"

I hold up my hand. "As friends though." I step forward. "Yeah. I'm willing to put aside what happened in college and move forward from this point on as coworkers *and* friends. I mean, not the kind that hang out all the time or anything, but two people who share a mutual past and work together."

"And what made you change your mind?" His cocky smirk is about to shine any moment, I can tell.

"It's too much work hating you all the time."

And there it is in all its glory. The cocky smirk women fawn over. "I am pretty likable, eh?"

"Yeah, eh?"

He rolls his eyes and shakes his head when I mock his Canadianism.

"But the ball's in your court, Lee. Do you think it's possible for us to be friends?" I'm feeling a little unsure because he hasn't actually told me he's still on board.

He's quiet for a moment. "It's a hard question to answer when you're wearing my clothes and sleeping at my condo, but…" His eyes scan down and up my body and he sighs. "Sorry, just one last time."

"Lee!" My nipples draw tight and I hope he can't see.

He laughs. "I think it's a good start."

Then he leaves the kitchen and walks down the hallway. I don't move, pondering what he means by that before deciding that maybe I'm better off playing dumb.

fifteen

. . .

Lee

It's our first preseason game today, and instead of having my head in the game, it's on Shayna.

Since the night she stayed at my place, there's been a shift between us. It's not like we're actual friends or anything—I mean, I'm not texting her or grabbing something to eat with her—but she doesn't turn around and go in the opposite direction when she sees me either. The energy wafting off her feels natural and no longer like she'd like to bury an axe in my head.

Which is great, right?

I mean, isn't that exactly what I wanted all along?

So I don't know why I feel as if I can have more from her. Even if she was willing, it's not like anything can happen between us with us both working for the Kingsmen. Not to mention the fact that my mind needs to be focused on being the best quarterback in the league to ensure the Kingsmen will sign me again.

Still, I'd be a liar if I said I didn't want her up against a wall, on my kitchen counter, in my bed. Pretty much any position she'd want to be in. And I'd be crazy if I said I didn't wonder if sometimes she feels the same. I'm sure when she acted as though she wanted to string me up by the balls that was genuine. But when I leaned past her to set the glass down and grab the towel, I saw disappointment in her eyes when I withdrew. If I didn't think I was crazy for saying so, I'd say she wished I would have made a move.

But that doesn't make any sense. And this is what consumes me more than the fucking playbook.

Needing to tape up my ankles, I head over to the trainers' area. Shayna is finishing up Darius, so I rush over to be next.

"All set?" she asks and pats the table without noticing it's me.

I slide on and she looks around as if people are gawking at us.

"Yep." I slide into position and stretch out my legs. I'm still wearing my basketball shorts.

She grabs the tape from a nearby table. Although I'll only get minutes with her, her hands will be touching me. God, I sound like a creep.

She straightens and widens her stance. "All right, let's do your left foot first."

Her delicate fingers grasp my ankle, tugging my foot forward. I should have had a conversation starter in mind. We're trying to be friends and friends talk about stuff with each other. She said she didn't want to be the kind of friends who text and hang out, but she also said she could never forgive me and look where we are now. I'm hopeful our friendship can grow into something more… when one of us moves to another team.

The truth is, I just like being around her. Simple as that.

"Did you ever find out where Bryce was last weekend?" I ask.

She doesn't look up at me, using all her concentration on where she's whipping the roll of tape around my leg, but one corner of her mouth creeps up. "I did."

When she doesn't offer anything else, I say, "And…"

"And it's none of your business."

She's a good secret keeper for her friend, since my assumption is Bryce went off with a player. "Ah, so she hooked up with someone."

Her gaze darts around the room, but she doesn't confirm or deny what I say. "I didn't say she hooked up."

I chuckle. "You didn't have to."

Shayna rolls her eyes, but it feels kind of playful, so again —progress.

The morning after the gala, she called the hotel and tracked down her purse. Apparently it had been swept up with the auction items, but the person who collected it noticed the next morning and returned it to the hotel's lost and found. I took her back to the hotel, then dropped her off at Bryce's since she'd returned home by then.

She sets down my left ankle and goes to my right. "How do you feel about today's game?"

I crack my neck a couple times. "I feel good. We should be able to beat Green Bay, but I always have nerves before a game."

Shayna nods. "Makes sense. It's the first time you're going to see how everyone works together in a game."

Her hair falls and tickles my left calf. My hand itches to tuck it behind her ear. "Exactly. Practice is one thing, but an actual game is something else entirely. Different players on the other side, more pressure, a stadium full of fans."

"Well, from what I've seen, you guys are ready." She smiles and gently sets my foot back on the table. "Let me see your right wrist."

She steps forward and I catch a whiff of her perfume. I inhale deeper, enjoying the floral scent while Shayna tapes my wrist.

"Make sure you really stretch out that hamstring before the game. And come see one of the trainers after so we can massage it out again and get you in an ice bath to reduce any inflammation."

I nod, knowing the protocol but fucking loving how concerned she is. My right hamstring has been tight all week through practice. It's probably from overuse—I've really been pushing myself ahead of this game—but a little discomfort is worth it if it helps me perform better.

"It's feeling better every day."

She moves to the other side of the table to tape my left wrist. "Good, that's what we like to hear."

"I'm calling dibs on Shayna," Elijah, one of our cornerbacks, says.

She looks over her shoulder and laughs. Then she rips the tape and squeezes the end onto me and steps back. "You're done. Have a great game."

Although she smiles, her eyes never quite reach mine.

She turns to Elijah. "You're up next."

As I lower myself from the table, it dawns on me that she's treating him with the same friendly professionalism she just treated me with, and that realization makes me bump shoulders with Elijah as we pass.

"What the fuck, Burrows?" he asks.

I make a sound that you'd think would come out of Chase and go to my locker to finish getting dressed for the game.

I always want more from Shayna. First it was for her to forgive me, then it was to be friends, and now that we're friends… do I want to be best friends? Because we sure as shit can't be anything more as long as we're both employed here.

Even I don't know the answer to that question, but I can't be bothered with it now. I have a job to do—I need to lead my team to victory and prove to them and everyone else that we have what it takes to make it to the Super Bowl.

———

We went 3-2 during preseason, and today is our first game of the season. The locker room is buzzing with energy.

I haven't seen Shayna much these past days. On the plane, she sat with the rest of the medical team. There's no official divide, but it would've been weird if I'd asked her to sit near me, or if I'd plopped down beside her away from the rest of the players.

And I didn't dare go to her to be taped today because I had her help me all three of the preseason games and I worried that maybe someone would notice.

"You ready for this?" Brady asks me once we're suited up.

I stand and we bump fists. "You know it. Plays?"

He's been a killer for us so far in the preseason. He knows our playbook, sure, but even when the plays go to shit, for some reason, we're on the same wavelength out there.

"It's all up here." He taps the side of his head.

"We're in trouble then," Chase says, joining us.

"Andrews." He bumps fists with us.

"Let's fuck'em up." Chase pounds a fist into Brady's other hand.

Chase is always a man of few words, but he can also be scary intense sometimes when it's game time. His dark-brown eyes are focused, and I'd be scared shitless if I were a wide receiver on the other team.

Coach comes in and peps us up with a few inspirational words. And then it's my job to get them going. After my speech, all the boys are yelling and we put our hands in.

I continue to lead the pack. "Who are we?"

"Kingsmen," the team answers.

"I can't fucking hear you. Who are we?"

"Kingsmen."

"What are we gonna do?"

"Win!" the team yells.

"Louder!" I demand.

"*Win!*" the team screams.

"Sure as fuck. Get your asses out there and beat the shit out of Chicago!"

The guys all jump and jog out of the locker room.

I lead the pack along with Miles and Brady because we're the captains. We walk down the hallway where some press lingers, snapping photos. The coaches and other staff members, like the medical team, wait for us to run out to the field before joining.

The announcer yells, "For our opposing team, we give you the San Francisco KINGSMEN!"

We storm out of the tunnel and onto Chicago's field. The roar of the crowd booing—since Chicago is known for loyal fans—gets me excited. Playing in front of all these people still gives me goose bumps.

The vibration of the noise soaks into my bones, gives me an adrenaline rush, and makes me feel as though I can do anything. Every year during the first game of the season it's the same—I'm filled with the sense that I belong here. I'm doing what I was meant to do and it only acts as extra motivation for me.

A glance toward the sideline and I spot Shayna, but I quickly turn away before she notices me staring. Or god help me, a camera. I have to remember how often the camera turns my way. I have to keep my head in the game, and that doesn't involve pining away for a woman who is happy with my friendship. Chicago is gonna make sure we work for this win.

Somehow, I do manage to keep my head in the game and we win 19-10.

I'm limping after the final play, my hamstring tight, so I head over to the medical staff to get stretched and massaged before my ice bath. My plan was to see Shayna, but Elijah's ass is already stretched out on her table and her hands are on his thigh.

He better not be trying to get her pants.

Since Shayna's not available, I go over to Randy because

he's stationed right beside her. How sad is this? I should be on the other side of the fucking room.

"How's the hammy?" Randy asks.

"Little tight. Not like earlier this week though. I may have strained it more on the last play."

"Anything else?" His fingers dig into my hamstring and it immediately feels better.

I consider telling him that my shoulder has been a little tender but think better of it. Randy wouldn't be the first over-enthusiastic athletic trainer to go overboard because of a little stiffness and pain. With it being early in the season, the medical team could absolutely pull me for a few games to see if it gets better.

Unless the shoulder starts to bother me more, I won't say anything. I can't let the upper office think I'm injured and expect them to sign me next year.

"Nah, just the hamstring." I catch Shayna looking at me dubiously from where she's working on Elijah.

"Good game, Burrows," Elijah says.

He and I have played together for a year, but we're not super close. Certainly not close enough for me to tell him to back the fuck off Shayna and not have him question me. He plays on the defensive line, so I don't work with him as much as the offensive team.

"Thanks, man. Killer deflection in the third. We needed that."

He smiles. "I have to say I love pissing off those wide receivers when they're concentrating only on the ball and here I come like a ninja out of the dark."

The whole room laughs.

Randy massages my hamstring, and while usually I'm talkative and would chat him up, today I remain quiet so that I hear Shayna and Elijah's conversation. It's nothing of impor-tance, but I wish her hands were on me and I was the center of her focus.

When I'm done, I hop off the table and thank Randy, then say bye to Shayna and Elijah. For some reason, she's still working on him.

After I strip down to my slider shorts, the stinging bite of the ice bath is a welcome distraction from the thoughts racing around my brain. Thoughts I shouldn't be having. Being jealous of my teammates talking to Shayna isn't an option for me.

Fuck. Maybe it's time I got laid. It's been a while—since before Shayna joined the team. Maybe that's my issue. I'm just horny in general and need to get off with a woman rather than my hand and memories of a woman I can't have. But if that's the case, how come none of the women I've come into contact with over the past couple of months have done anything for me?

As I'm about to leave the locker room, my cell rings and my brother's name flashes on the screen.

"Hey, Kane. What's up?"

"Great game you had today."

"You watched?" I wave goodbye to a couple of the guys leaving the locker room.

"I always watch, you know that."

I chuckle. "True, but you're a newlywed. I'm surprised you came up for air long enough to see the game."

"I didn't say I saw every second of it." The amusement in his voice is good to hear. There were times I worried he'd live his life alone and lonely with his dog.

"Spare me the details."

"Seriously, though. You looked good out there. I have a good feeling about this season for you."

Jana, his bride, says good game in the background.

"How do you feel about your own season?" I ask.

My brother is a retired professional hockey player, but now he coaches the Florida Fury hockey team, while his new wife is the team's owner.

"You worry about football, and I'll handle hockey."

Once my dad died and my mom fell into her depression, then went in and out of mental health facilities every time she became suicidal, Kane raised me. He didn't take a scholarship down in the States, but stayed up by us in British Columbia to get me through high school. So although he doesn't have to worry about me anymore, it's ingrained in him.

"Fair enough." I head toward the locker room exit so that I can get on the bus back to the hotel.

Kane's quiet for a moment, and I hear Jana whispering.

"If she's blowing you and you're talking…"

"Fuck off," he says. "Um… I also wanted to call and check in on that other situation."

I don't need to ask him to clarify. He's asking about Shayna.

"It's better. Not exceptional, but better than it was." I stop short when I spot Shayna at the end of the hall. She almost looks as if she's waiting for me.

"Glad to hear it," Kane says. "I thought maybe her presence would be a distraction, but your game tonight didn't show that at all."

I stop walking and stand in front of Shayna.

Seeing that I'm on the phone, she whispers, "Can I talk to you for a second?"

Nodding, I say into the receiver, "What was it you just told me? I'll worry about football, and you worry about hockey?"

"Touché," he says with a laugh.

"Listen, I gotta run. I'll call you later?"

"Yep. I just wanted to touch base. Call whenever you can."

"Will do." I hang up and shove the phone in my pocket. "Sorry, my brother."

She nods. "He plays professional hockey, right?"

"Yeah, coach now. Florida Fury."

Shayna looks uncomfortable and hesitant to talk to me about whatever she was waiting on me for.

"Everything okay?"

She nods toward an empty room to her right. "Can we talk in there?"

My forehead wrinkles. "Sure… everything okay?"

I follow her into the room. She closes the door then turns to face me.

"I'm hoping that's what you'll tell me," she says.

I tilt my head.

"Your throwing arm shoulder? How long has it been bothering you?" She crosses her arms, and I sense that this conversation will be more like an interrogation than a conversation.

And here I thought maybe she wanted to shove her tongue down my throat in congratulations for the win. But no, that remains my fantasy.

sixteen

. . .

Shayna

"What are you talking about?" he asks with a scowl he's never faced me with.

I'm not imagining the way the corner of his mouth turned up, just for a moment, almost like a grimace, with every long pass.

"Don't bullshit me, Lee. I heard Randy ask you if anything else was bothering you. Why didn't you mention your shoulder?" I cross my arms.

"Because there's nothing wrong with it."

"You're lying to me."

My words seem to hit him like a slap in the face. Maybe because his lying is what caused problems between us all those years ago.

"I know my body, Shayna, and I'm fine." He moves to push past me, and I instinctively step in his path, putting my hand on his chest to prevent him from leaving.

He's back in the suit he wore to the game—dark navy with a white shirt, collar open—and damn if he doesn't look delectable. His hot, hard chest under my palm causes me to step closer. We stand, eyes locked with my hand still on his chest, almost breathing each other in before I clear my throat and retract my hand.

"You can trust me. Tell me what's going on."

He heaves out a pained sigh and turmoil swirls in his eyes. "Please don't press this, Shayna." His voice is begging and quiet as if the walls have ears.

"If something is bothering you, you need to let the medical staff help." I lower my voice, hoping he'll notice that I understand how confidential this issue needs to be.

He shakes his head before I'm even done speaking. "No. I've seen them pull guys for less on a just-in-case basis. We're at the beginning of the season. My contract ends this year. The team needs me. I'm fine."

"Lee—"

"Just drop it, okay?" This time, he does push past me. I turn, hoping he changes his mind. He stops with his hand on the door, back still facing me. "You have my word that if it becomes something, I'll tell someone, but please, Shayna, this stays here."

Frowning, I stare at the closed door long after he's left. I don't know what to think. Or what to do for that matter.

Protocol dictates that I report my suspicions to the team doctor, but some sort of weird loyalty to Lee keeps me quiet, because instead of turning left to head back to the team area to find Dr. Carlisle, I turn right to leave and head back to the hotel.

Two weeks have passed since my confrontation with Lee in Chicago, and he's studiously avoided me as much as possible. I don't know why. I'm not the enemy. In fact, it's the opposite —I'm trying to look out for him.

I'm not wrong, something is going on with his shoulder.

Even if he hadn't basically admitted as much to me, I see every grimace.

I'm surprised no one else on the medical team has picked up on it. The way his mouth twitches, how he doesn't quite fully extend his arm back when he's throwing. The difference is minuscule, but it's there.

Maybe I've spent too much time staring at him over the years and that's why I'm picking up on it, I don't know. But the man is a stubborn ass. There's a good chance this problem isn't going to just magically go away if he ignores it. If we identify the problem and treat it, he has a much better chance at a positive outcome and playing this season.

Knowing that I'm right about his shoulder, I'm pissed when I find Lee working out on a Friday night after a week full of conditioning and practices.

We leave for Denver tomorrow ahead of Sunday's game, so I'm at the training facility to get a workout in because I'll be tied up all weekend. It's becoming harder and harder to find the time to work out these days.

"Wasn't expecting to find you here." I head over to one of the treadmills and turn it on.

He lets the dumbbells fall to the floor with a bang.

"Why? It's happened before." He's breathing heavily.

I glance at the weights and see that he's lifting about twenty pounds more than he should.

"Just because of your... you know." I point at my right shoulder.

He looks around. There's no one else here except for Paul the security guard. "Jesus, are you still on that? I told you, I'm fine."

"I heard what you said. I just don't believe you." I increase the speed on the treadmill so that I'm doing a relaxed jog, drowning out his lies.

He leaves the weight area and stomps over to the treadmill. "Would you give it a break already? Have you considered the fact that you might be wrong?"

I shrug. "For about a second. But I know I'm not."

He stabs the stop button on my treadmill, and it slowly comes to a stop.

"Hey!" I shift to face him. With me on the treadmill and him on the ground, we're almost the same height.

"I need to get some extra time in. We lost our second game, and I don't like losing. I really don't like losing on a year when my contract is coming up."

I shake my head. He can't really be this shortsighted. "Lee, you need to take this seriously. Just tell me what's going on and maybe—"

"I told you. If there's something you need to know, I'll tell you."

"Like you told me about the bet?" I don't know why I'm attacking him about that again. The words just slipped out from sheer anger that he's lying right to my face. It's not omission this time. He's straight up lying to me.

He throws up his hands. "Jesus, this again? I thought we moved past that."

I shake my head. "I'm sorry. I shouldn't have said that."

"I give up. I can't fucking do anything right in your eyes." He steps up onto my treadmill so he's once again towering over me. I don't know if it's an intimidation tactic or what, but I refuse to let it work if that's what he's angling for.

"I said I'm sorry. It just doesn't make sense to me why you're hiding an injury."

He steps closer to me. "It's not an injury, it's just a little discomfort. Nothing I can't handle."

I rise on my tiptoes and stand as straight as I can. "You stubborn fool. You know as well as I do that ignoring a small injury is the first step to making it a big injury. It could turn into something that needs surgery." My hands are clenched in fists at my sides.

Our chests are millimeters from touching and my breasts heave with my heavy breaths.

"It's not something you need to concern yourself with," he grinds out between gritted teeth.

"I think it is."

Electricity crackles in the small space between us.

"You're so frustrating sometimes!" He pushes a hand through his sweaty hair.

"Ha! Look who's talking!" I poke him in the chest.

We stare at each other, our chests rising and falling. We're so close that I smell his minty breath. My lips tingle when his gaze dips down to them and I fight not to moan when his tongue slides along his bottom lip.

His head dips, my head rises, and all of a sudden his lips are on mine and my hands are pushing into his sweaty hair. He plunges his tongue into my mouth, not waiting for an invitation. I open to him with a moan, arching my chest to press against his when his tongue strokes mine.

God, he tastes just like I remember.

I pull back for a moment and look him square in the eyes. "This changes nothing."

"I know." Then his lips crash against mine again and his arm wraps around my waist, pulling me flush to his body.

Just like in college, I lose myself completely in him. The rest of the world fades away—the fact that what we're doing is forbidden, the fact that we're in a team facility, the fact that this is a spectacularly bad idea.

I've already proven to myself that I easily fall into the rabbit hole that is Lee Burrows, and even if he has changed, I don't ever want someone to control my feelings like he did back then. Relying on this man for my happiness will only lead to heartbreak.

With that thought, I unwind my hands from his hair and push against his chest.

He doesn't try to prolong the kiss, and he lets me step back from him.

I stare at him with wide eyes, lips still tingling.

He opens his mouth to say something, but I can't hear what he's going to say and still walk away from him.

"That was a mistake." I push past him.

He must agree because he doesn't fight me, but rather squeezes to the side of the treadmill, allowing me to pass. I rush over to where I left my bag and race out of there as though the devil is chasing me.

seventeen

. . .

Lee

Shayna's the one avoiding me now. You'd think she was the president from how many times I've tried to get her alone to apologize to her for kissing her last week.

She surrounds herself with people all the time, and when we're done with practice for the day, she races out of the building before I can chase her. Bryce was here earlier this week to interview some of the players, and when I asked her if she could pass along Shayna's number, she looked at me as though I'd asked her if she knew where I could buy meth.

Whatever, none of that matters. It's game day again and we're in Los Angeles. We only have seventeen regular season games, so we have to make every single one of them count. I don't want us going into next week down two games this season.

We perform decently during the first half, the score zero to eight, but our luck is about to change early in the third. We have possession of the ball. It's fourth down with five yards to go to score our first down, and I call a play that has Brady faking left but then breaking off right to catch my pass.

It's risky. We could try to run the ball, but Los Angeles's

offensive line has been tight this afternoon and we're better off trying to move the ball up the field with a pass.

Our center snaps the ball to me and I pretend to look left, the direction we want Los Angeles to think Brady is headed. When he breaks right, one of the Los Angeles players is on him and manages to stay between Brady and me.

I pull my arm back to throw but hold on to the ball a beat to see if Brady can get into a better position. The last thing we can afford is a fucking interception right now.

Finally, Brady gets in a better position and I snap my arm all the way back and throw the ball. A sharp pain stabs my arm, then one of Los Angeles's players tackles me from the right.

The crowd roars but quiets down, seeing that I'm sprawled out on the field, clutching my right shoulder, rocking back and forth.

My Kingsmen teammates gather around me and call for medical to come out on the field.

Miles kneels beside me, concern overfilling his eyes. "What happened?"

"My fucking shoulder." I move my arm and groan when a lightning bolt of pain races up my arm and through my shoulder.

"Just take it easy." He looks to the sidelines. "Frampton's coming."

Seconds later, Dr. Frampton appears by my side, along with some of the other more senior medical staff. "Talk to me, Lee."

"I don't know. It's my right shoulder. Lots of pain, worse when I move it. *Fuck!*" I scream and not from the pain but the fact I'm about to be taken out of this game on an injury.

He touches my shoulder, and I wince. "Let's get you off the field so we can check you out. Do you think you can sit up if we support you on your left side?"

"Yeah, yeah, I think so."

He comes along the other side of me, and with Miles's help, they get me standing to walk off the field. My face twists in pain at the inevitable movement of my right arm. Once I'm standing, the crowd claps to show their support and I raise my left hand in acknowledgment.

All I can think about are Shayna's words at the gym—*it could turn into something major that needs surgery.*

Damn it. Anger heats my face, and if I had the ability, I'd punch a wall to dispel the rage building inside me. I don't even know if I'm angry with myself, the guy who hit me, or the teammate who let our opponent tackle me.

Shayna's on the sidelines, and instead of a smug "I told you so" look, there's nothing but concern in her gaze.

Because we both know this is the "something major" she warned me about, and I have no one to blame but myself.

"How bad is it?" Joran asks as soon as I answer his call.

I would've thought my agent would be the first to call, but Kane beat him to it last night.

"They did an X-ray last night to make sure nothing is broken and that came back clear. I have to go for an MRI. Right now, my arm is in a fucking sling."

Miles glances at me. He offered to drive me to the medical center since I can't even get myself from *A* to *B* right now.

"What the hell happened? Was it that piece of shit who sacked you?"

My mouth presses into a thin line. "I don't know what it was. Guess we'll see what it is and go from there."

"Jesus. This is not good, Lee."

I'm so not in the mood for him right now. I grip the phone tighter. "You think I don't know that? You think I want to be benched?"

Joran blows out a breath. "You're right, I know, I know. It's just hard to negotiate a contract for an injured player. You need to call me the second you find out what's wrong and how long you'll be out." He hangs up without saying good-bye, which is just who he is, but where was the fucker last night.

"This is fucking hell." My head falls back against the headrest of Miles's Tesla.

"Listen, we've got the best of the best about to look at your shoulder. They're going to tell you what's going on and how to get you back out on the field the fastest."

He's right. One of the perks of being in our profession is the spectacular sports medical care we receive, but there's only so much they can do. There're things they can't control, like your healing time and how your body cooperates.

"I can't believe I'm in this fucking position." I slam my left fist down on the console.

"Hey, man. Ease up." He runs his hand down the center console. "Destroy your own shit."

"Sorry," I mumble.

"It's okay, I know you're good for it if you break it." He smiles.

We drive in silence until we reach the treatment facility. Another perk to my job is I can get in at a moment's notice, where others would have to go to a hospital for this kind of diagnostic test.

I tell Miles thanks and to take off while I undergo the MRI and wait for the results, but he makes up the excuse that he wanted to get a light workout in anyway, so he'll just wait until I'm done so he can drop me off at home afterward.

I should've expected as much. Miles has a tendency to act like a big brother to everyone, not just Twyla.

The MRI doesn't take long, then the team doctors take a look at my arm, checking my range of motion, then they go off to look at the X-rays again and review the MRI results.

I'm sitting in Coach's office, waiting for them to return,

shooting the shit about what went wrong in the game yesterday—both when I was on and off the field—while he squeezes a stress ball. Dr. Frampton and Dr. Carlisle walk in with drawn faces. Bile rises up my throat because I know without them even opening their mouths that the news isn't good.

"Just say it," I grate out.

They look from me to Coach and back again.

There's a knock on the door before they can say anything, and the team owner, Giles Hanover, walks in. "What are we looking at?" he says by way of greeting.

He was obviously called the minute my injury was clear. It's bad enough I failed myself with this injury, but I've failed the men in this room too, as well as the entire team.

Dr. Frampton's face is tight, and it's clear to me he knows that no one in this room will like what he has to say. "Lee has a Grade II AC joint injury, probably as a result of when he was tackled. There's also a very small tear on the rotator cuff. We can treat that with some ice and anti-inflammatories, but it should heal on its own by the time he's back on the field."

I swallow hard. "How long am I out?"

Every second that ticks by before I get my answer feels like a goddamn month.

"Hard to say, but likely somewhere between four to five weeks," Dr. Frampton says.

"Fuck!" Coach tosses the stress ball across the room while Giles stands there with his hands on his hips, frowning.

"I can't get out there any sooner?" I look between Dr. Frampton and Dr. Carlisle.

"It's unlikely," Dr. Carlisle says. "You'll need to be completely immobilized in a sling for the first week. From there, we'll do some more imaging and slowly start building back your strength. When we see what you can tolerate, that will give us more information."

Every word out of his mouth is like a dagger piercing my heart.

Giles looks at Coach. "You think Hayes can hold it down until Lee returns?"

Hayes is the backup quarterback, and not to sound like an asshole, but he's not me. Sure, he played Division One, drafted high on the order. He wouldn't be signed to the team if he weren't, but I'm the guy who's supposed to lead the team to the Bowl this year.

Dr. Frampton must see something in my face and take pity on me because he says, "Lee, let's head back to my office. I want to check your sling and go over a few things you're going to need to do over the next week."

When I leave the room, Coach and Giles are talking about how they're going to get Hayes ready for this weekend's game. It's a stark reminder of how replaceable you are in this business. Loyalty only goes as far as what you can offer the team, and if I want to remain a Kingsmen next year when my contract is up, I need to prove my worth. Which means healing as fast as I possibly can.

eighteen

. . .

Shayna

The news about Lee's shoulder is all over every sports channel even before I make it to the training facility to read the official report that verifies most of what they're saying.

It's been a couple of days since Lee was benched, and I haven't seen him. He's been told to rest, keep his right arm immobile, and eat whatever the nutrition team sends over to him to help speed up healing and reduce inflammation.

Half of me still wants to avoid him because of our kiss, and the other half of me feels compelled to check on him because I'm sure he's probably not dealing well with this injury.

"What's got your face all twisted?" Bryce says beside me in the back of our Uber.

"Just work stuff."

She blows out a breath and eyes me skeptically. "You mean a certain quarterback?"

"I didn't say that."

"You didn't have to," she says dryly. "This is exactly why I'm making you do this."

By this, she means forcing me out on a double date. She

met some guy in line at the coffee shop earlier this week and arranged for me to meet his friend.

"You need to put *him* and that kiss in the rearview mirror." She takes out her lipstick and applies another coat while looking into the camera app of her phone.

It's not that I think she's wrong. I know she's right. But I can't stop wondering where Lee's head is at—on both the kiss and his injury.

"You're right. I'm sorry." I squeeze her hand. "Thanks for making me do this. Maybe Will's friend will be my Mister Right."

"Or just a good distraction." She chuckles.

One thing I've learned about Bryce is that she doesn't take her dating life very seriously. She goes through guys like a '90s stockbroker goes through lines of cocaine. I'm envious of her because she never gets weighed down emotionally when one of her short-lived relationships ends.

And here I am, still thinking about a guy from college.

I need to get a life.

We pull up in front of the restaurant that's been built onto the side of a whiskey distillery. A patio outside has hanging lights that zigzag overhead, and music is pumping out of speakers. It's the top end of casual, so I'm wearing dark jeans with heels and a silk cami and leather jacket.

We thank the Uber driver, then head inside and approach the hostess.

"Welcome to Rock Hard Whiskey. Do you have a reservation?"

Bryce smiles. "I believe it should be under William. For four?"

The hostess checks her computer then smiles and picks up some menus. "The reservation was made for the patio. Does that still work?"

Bryce looks at me, and I nod. It's a little cool, but I have my jacket and I saw that they have several infrared heaters spread throughout the patio, so it should be fine.

"That works," Bryce says.

The hostess leads us through the restaurant and out a set of roll-up doors onto the patio, where she sets the menus on an empty table and tells us our server will be with us shortly to take our drink orders.

"Our first double date." Bryce's dark eyes flare with anticipation.

I chuckle. "You're very excited for a casual dinner date. Do you really like this guy?"

She waves me off. "No, I'm excited to be out with you. The dick is just a bonus."

I bark out a sharp laugh and glance around to see if anyone heard her, but they're all involved in their own conversations. Plus the music probably drowned her out.

We chat for a few minutes until the hostess leads a pair of men to our table. They're both in jeans and casual button-downs. The dark-haired one I know is William because Bryce showed me his picture on Instagram. And the one with the dark-blond hair and blue eyes must be his friend, Bennett.

"Hey there, gorgeous." William kisses Bryce's cheek and she smiles up at him.

"Hello to you too. This is my friend Shayna." She motions to me across the table.

William extends his hand, and I accept it. "Pleasure to meet you, Shayna. This is my best friend, Bennett."

Bennett shakes my hand and sits beside me, looking me directly in the eyes. "Pleasure."

He has beautiful blue eyes. The light ones that are almost transparent. The ones women go crazy over. Unfortunately, every woman but me, because I want hazel eyes with green specks. Those are the color eyes that I go crazy over.

The waiter approaches before we have a chance to start a conversation, and we each place our drink order.

"Sorry we're a few minutes late. My street is getting road work done, so they have it blocked off and we had to walk a few blocks to meet up with the Uber," Bennett says.

"That sounds like way too much effort," Bryce says. "I probably would've just canceled."

I smother a laugh because I'm almost positive she's not joking.

"Where do you live?" I ask him.

"Cow Hollow," he says as though I should know where that is.

"Sorry, I just moved to the area, so I'm not that familiar with all the different neighborhoods."

He smiles. "Oh okay, it's pretty much south of the marina and to the west of Russian Hill… if you know where that is."

I picture Lee in his condo in Russian Hill. Lying in bed and wearing those blue pajama pants without a shirt. I push that thought out of my mind. "All right, I have some kind of idea where that is now."

"You said you just moved to the area. What brought you here?"

"A job. I just started with the Kingsmen as an athletic trainer."

He blinks a couple of times. "Wow, that's amazing. I'll bet that's an interesting job. Do you have to travel with the team to all their away games?"

I nod and we chat while Bryce and William carry on their own conversation. I learn that Bennett is a California native but moved up here from San Diego eight years ago when he took a job with a tech start-up company. He has two sisters and is the baby of the family, and his parents are divorced.

By the time the waiter comes over with our drinks and takes our food order, I've decided that although Bennett is an attractive man who seems somewhat charming, it's not a love match. There's no spark.

Of course, there won't be any love matches until a certain

someone gets out of my head, and I have no idea how to go about doing that.

Regardless, I decide to give this date my all. Who knows? Maybe by the end of dinner, there will be a magic spark of romance between Bennett and me. God knows I'd welcome it.

nineteen

. . .

Lee

The universe has a sick sense of humor.

Miles is a great best friend, but he's been a thorn in my side lately. He's so hell-bent on preventing me from falling into some depression, he's been at my place more than his own since my injury. And then he planned this dinner with some of the guys to get me out of the house. I have no desire whatsoever to be here, but Brady insisted that Hard Rock distillery has better whiskey than what is served at other bars and restaurants around the city, that they keep their good stuff only at their place. Cole Webber, his family friend, told him so. Although I'm not supposed to be drinking, a nice stiff drink is the only thing that sounds good tonight.

So here I am with Miles, Chase, Brady—and apparently Shayna... and her date.

Because sure as shit, when I glance at the patio, I have a perfect view of Shayna on what appears to be a double date with Bryce. But she's too wrapped up in her conversation with the Ken doll lookalike sitting beside her to notice me.

"You hear me, Burrows?"

Brady's voice drags me back to where my attention should be.

"Sorry, what'd you say?" With my good arm, I bring my drink to my lips and down a decent-sized swig.

"I asked whether medical has told you what day you're gonna get the sling off."

"After this Sunday's game. They have to run some more tests first to confirm." I take another swig. Brady's right. Whatever he asked for when the waitress came is the best whiskey I've ever tasted.

"You'll be back on the field in no time," Miles says. He gives me a look that says if I believe it, it will happen.

"I fucking hope so. Sitting around doing nothing all day isn't for me. Fuck retirement, they'll have to drag me off the field before I stop playing."

Brady shrugs. "Hey now. You can settle down, start a family?"

"We can't all be number one, dad," Chase grumbles.

I met Brady's son, Theo, at practice last week. That kid has buckets of energy and goes like the Energizer Bunny. I don't know how Brady can split his focus between his son and the game, but I give him props for being so involved in his kid's life. God knows I would've appreciated having a parent like him when I was growing up.

I glance at Shayna's table as she throws her head back and laughs. Is that who does it for her these days? A fucking comedian?

"You're right. There can only be one of us to hold that distinction." Brady grins and takes a pull from his beer. "None of you ever think of getting serious with anyone?" He looks around the table at the three of us.

I can't help the way my gaze darts to Shayna at his question.

Miles sits directly across from me and must notice that my attention is divided because he glances over his shoulder and turns to look back at me, then back at her table, then back at me with a frown. He's obviously spotted Shayna.

"Not a fucking chance," Chase says.

"You'd have to get more words in your vocabulary and a personality first," Brady jokes.

Chase scowls. Nothing new there.

"Chase has a personality," I say. "It's just buried under fifty pounds of aggression."

Everyone laughs but Chase. We're always riding him for being so grumpy all the time—it's like everything in existence annoys him—but he couldn't care less.

Movement on the patio drags my attention away as Shayna gets up from the table. My eyes track her as she enters the restaurant. She must be heading to the restroom because she beelines it to the back and disappears down the hallway.

"I gotta hit the head." I push my chair back and stand.

Miles looks over his shoulder again and turns to me as I'm walking away. "Lee..."

I ignore him and keep walking until I'm standing outside the women's washroom. It takes everything in me not to go in.

A couple minutes later, she steps out into the hall.

"Shayna."

She startles and whips around with her hand on her chest to face me where I stand at the end of the hallway. "Lee? What are you doing here?"

"Having dinner with some of the guys." I step out of the darkness. "What are you doing?"

She fidgets with the hem of her cami and shuffles her feet a few times. Her chin tips up slightly and her jaw takes a hard edge. "I'm here on a date. Which I think, for some reason, you already know."

I shrug and take another step toward her. "Yeah, I saw."

We stare at each other for a moment. She's daring me to say something when we both know I have no right. But the words are on the tip of my tongue. I want to tear that asshole she's sitting with limb from limb for even breathing the same air as her, for making her laugh, for getting to be the one she's here with tonight.

"Is it serious?"

Shayna's eyes narrow. "Not that it's any of your business, but it's our first date."

Her admittance gives me a small amount of relief.

When her gaze flicks to my sling, I'm reminded that we haven't seen each other since my injury.

"How's your shoulder?" There's real concern in her tone. What I don't know is whether it's because she's paid to be concerned or whether she's concerned because it's me.

"Brutal. Can't do a fucking thing with this sling on."

She frowns. "You'll get it off soon. Then you can start working to get back on the field."

"Yeah, well, that feels like a really long time right about now."

Her hand reaches out, but she retracts it before she touches me. "The entire medical team is going to do everything in our power to help you get back to the level of performance you were at before the injury. Just try to take this time to let your body heal."

Jesus, this is not the conversation I want to be having with her right now.

"I want to talk about the kiss," I blurt.

I've wanted to talk about the kiss every day since it happened, but Shayna made it pretty clear that she didn't.

Jesus, getting my lips back on hers again was a special sort of torture. If I thought for a minute that it would sate my need and help me to stop thinking about her, it did the exact opposite. It was even better than I remembered. Everything about Shayna is a fucking turn-on to me—from the way she looks, to the way she smells, the way she tastes, the way she moves.

"We're not talking about that." She goes to spin around to leave, but I snag her wrist with my good hand.

"It happened for a reason."

She whips back around, face red with irritation. "It shouldn't have happened. And it won't happen again."

Fuck. Fuck!

I hate that she's right. It's against the Kingsmen's fraternization policy, and beyond that, having her back in my bed would only complicate things for me at work. But Jesus, after that kiss, being with anyone else is a waste of my time. Shayna is my one.

I release her wrist and she takes that as her signal to walk away. She stomps down the hall, and I head back to my table.

"Was that Shayna I just saw go out to the patio?" Brady asks.

"You're a fucking stalker now, Burrows?" Chase asks. "You're always following her to the bathroom. It's creepy."

Miles looks at me with something akin to "I told you you were screwed."

I blow out a breath then pick up my drink and toss back the rest. I glance around the three guys at the table.

I can trust them. I know I can. The question is whether I want to open this particular can of worms with them. But I'm desperate for advice. I need to talk to someone about what I'm feeling, and Kane is always the fatherly figure when he offers me his advice. Pushing down my need for Shayna is not making it go away. Maybe talking about it will get me further.

"Truth is…" I glance at Miles, who has the concerned dad look, silently asking me if I really want to do this. "I know Shayna from college."

I tell them about the stupid bet and how it ruined what we started, but I don't tell them about the kiss the other night. I can't out Shayna for that because it's against policy. The crux of the issue is that I want this woman in my bed something fierce, but I can't have her.

The entire time I'm talking, Miles is looking at me as though he knows there's more to the story. And maybe he does. He's known me the longest and is my closest friend. Saw me at my highest with Shayna and at my lowest when she dumped me. Perhaps I'm that transparent.

"Surprised she even took the job," Chase says when I finish.

I shrug. "It was a good opportunity for her, and I'm sure from her perspective, she probably thought 'I'm not gonna let that asshole ruin anything else for me.'"

Brady chuckles. "Yeah, I can see that."

"So what are you going to do?" Miles asks, watching me carefully.

I shrug. "Keep dealing with blue balls? I dunno."

"You can't fuck around with her. You know that, right?" Chase's intense gaze makes me shift uncomfortably in my seat.

"Haven't you been listening? That's the whole problem."

Chase shakes his head at me with a look of disgust. "There's more to life than pussy. Get over it."

I lean in a bit toward him. "I take it you've never had pussy like Shayna's then."

The words are crude and Shayna would castrate me if she overheard me, but I'm making a point.

He guffaws. "Had lots of pussy, man, and you know it. One's no different than the next."

I shake my head. I can't wait until some woman has Chase so twisted up inside he can't think of fucking anyone but her. Then I'll be the one laughing.

"Have you thought of sleeping with someone else?" Miles asks, but really he's changing the subject before Chase and I get into a pissing match.

"Yeah, you know what they say—best way to get over

someone is to get under someone else," Brady says. "Or behind them." He grins and waggles his eyebrows. "Or have them under you." His head moves right and left as though he could go on forever.

"Of course I've thought of that. I just can't get any motivation to act on it." I grip my glass, hating how much control Shayna has over me.

"Well then, you're fucked," Chase says matter-of-factly.

I raise my glass. "Cheers to that."

twenty

. . .

Shayna

I listen intently while Dr. Carlisle talks over the game plan for the week—listing the injuries from yesterday's game and discussing what protocols need to be taken, who's doing what today. Lastly, we discuss Lee's expected return.

Nothing is official yet—he's getting another MRI and X-ray right now—but he's expected to be able to lose the sling and start his rehabilitation today.

The Kingsmen squeaked out a win against Los Angeles last week, but part of that win is attributed to Lee sitting on the sidelines, offering Hayes words of wisdom during the game. As expected, the higher-ups are all eager for Lee to return as soon as possible.

Once Dr. Carlisle dismisses us, I head to the practice field along with some of my colleagues.

I'm about two hours into my day when Randy tells me that Dr. Carlisle needs me in the rehab room. My forehead wrinkles, but I thank him and head that way. When I enter the room, there are a couple of players who sustained some minor injuries during yesterday's game working with some trainers, and Dr. Carlisle and Lee stand at the far end.

My stomach churns as I make my way across the large

room. Did Dr. Carlisle somehow find out that Lee and I kissed? Did Lee tell him about our past for some reason? A million ideas run through my head while I slowly approach with a wide smile.

"You wanted to see me, Dr. Carlisle?" I purposely don't make eye contact with Lee.

My boss's mouth is tight and his face is drawn. "We have something to discuss."

I barely swallow, my mouth is so dry from nerves. "Okay…"

"Lee's results show a marked improvement in both the AC joint and the tear. He'll need another follow-up run of tests a week from now, but we've cleared him to remove the sling and do some light work this week to regain mobility and rebuild some strength."

I glance at Lee, who's watching me intently. I still don't understand why I was dragged in here. "That's great news."

"I'd made arrangements for Lee to work with one of the other trainers, but he insisted *you* help him with his rehab." The way he says it makes it clear what he thinks of the idea.

My eyes go wide. Why? Why would Lee do this? Is he trying to make people suspicious of us?

"Yes, that was my reaction too, but he wouldn't back down." He looks at Lee a little derisively, but Lee ignores him.

"I've seen you working with some of the other players and you seem like you know what you're doing. Elijah always speaks very highly of you." Lee has got to be kidding me.

"You're certain about this?" Dr. Carlisle asks in a tight voice.

Lee's voice is steel. "I already told you—I'm confident Shayna will be able to get me back in top condition. Right, Shayna?" He looks at me.

"Yeah, of course, absolutely." I awkwardly stumble over my words.

Dr. Carlisle sighs. "Fine. Get started today. I've gone ahead and put the rehab plan in the computer. You can find it there." He walks away, clearly annoyed things aren't going the way he wanted them to.

I wait for him to leave, and once he's gone, I whip around to face Lee. "What the hell are you doing?" I whisper.

He shrugs with his good shoulder. "I want the best of the best helping me. There's nothing more to it."

I narrow my eyes. "I haven't been with the team long enough for you to know whether I'm the best of the best."

He takes a small step forward, leaning down toward me. "But I've known you long enough to know that you put one hundred percent into everything you do and that nothing short of success will be good enough for you."

I have no answer to his compliments, so I don't address them. "This better not be some ploy to—"

"Relax, Shayna. You made it clear you regret what happened, and even if you didn't, I realize it's not an idea we can entertain. I simply want to get back on the field to help get this team to the playoffs." He holds my gaze and appears sincere enough, so I agree.

"Fine. Let me go look up what Dr. Carlisle has set for the treatment plan and we'll get started."

"Can't wait."

His grin reminds me of the boy from college, but I shake that thought loose. There's definitely no room for us to entertain those feelings now.

"Why don't you go get changed and I'll meet you back here? Be prepared to work."

"You're the boss."

I can't help but watch him leave the room, hoping no one notices the longing in my eyes.

"Seriously, one more?" Lee cringes as he completes another set.

"Do your fans know you're this much of a complainer?" I take the small free weight from him and return it to the weight rack.

"Do your friends know you're this much of a sadist?"

I laugh and walk over to one of the tables and pat it. "Hop up. We're not done yet."

Surprisingly, working with Lee hasn't been that bad. He hasn't tried to hit on me or bring up our past, the kiss, or our run-in at the restaurant when I was on a date. In some ways, spending time with him today reminds me of when I tutored him in college. I'd be all business and he'd do his best to steer us off course.

Lee walks over, and from the way he's holding his shoulder, it's sore. He might be super fit, but when your body is used to this kind of conditioning, even a week off requires building up your endurance again, especially after an injury.

"Lie on your back. I'm going to help stretch you out."

He gets up on the table and does as I say. Everyone else is long gone, back on the field for practice, so it's just the two of us in the rehab room.

I raise his leg slightly off the table and go through a series of stretches.

"Do you think it will really be three more weeks until I can get back on the field?" he asks.

I frown. There's no good answer. Every athlete and injury is different and there's no way to say for sure.

"I'll tell you what… we'll both do our parts and commit to getting you back out there as soon as possible, sound good?"

He blows out a frustrated breath. "That's a blow-off answer."

"What did your brother say? I'm sure he's had to deal with injuries over the course of his career. He must have had good advice for you."

A soft grunt leaves his lips as I push a little harder into the stretch. "He pretty much told me what everyone else has—do what the doctors say. Rest when I'm supposed to, then work my ass off in rehab to get back out there."

I lift a shoulder. "He's a smart man."

"It's not the physical part I'm struggling with."

"The mental?" I release his leg and walk around the table to work on his other side.

"Yeah. Believe it or not, this is the first time I've had to miss more than one game and I guess I wasn't prepared for how much it's fucking with my head." He's staring at me stretching him out, but I see his vulnerability. I wish I had magical advice that would make him feel better.

I pick up his other leg and begin the series of stretches. "There's a lot of pressure coming at you from a lot of different angles. That can't be easy for anyone to deal with."

A sardonic chuckle leaves his lips. "True. But honestly, most of it comes from my own head. It's like… if I can't perform on the football field, what good am I?"

I pause what I'm doing and look at him. "Lee, you're more than just your stats on the field. Nobody is just one thing."

He's quiet and contemplative for a moment, and I go back to the stretching.

"I guess… I don't know, doesn't matter."

My forehead wrinkles. "No, what were you going to say?"

He's closing up, and I don't want him keeping things locked inside.

Lee blows out a long breath. "I don't know what I told you back in college about my family life…" He lets the words hang there for a moment.

I shake my head. "Nothing really."

"Well, my dad died when I was pretty young, and it sort of sent my mom into a tailspin of depression and anxiety. Kane basically had to step in to raise me. He made sure to play close to home instead of taking a scholarship to the

States until I finished high school. My mom was an absentee parent, and when I was young, I used to work so hard to try to gain her attention, her praise—hell, any kind of emotion would've been welcome. Anything to acknowledge the fact that she knew I was there."

It's not unusual for athletes to use physical therapy as a form of emotional therapy too. Before I started with the Kingsmen, the athletes I worked with at the private practice in Wisconsin were always confessing all kinds of things to me. I think that something about being vulnerable physically allowed them to be vulnerable emotionally.

Usually, I can keep myself one step removed from whatever they're telling me, but listening to Lee tell me about his childhood makes my chest tighten. My family had its financial struggles, but at least my mom was present in my life.

"I'm sorry, Lee. That must've been very difficult." I set his leg down but stay where I am.

"Yeah, it sucked. I don't even know why I'm complaining —it was so long ago."

I rest my hand on his good shoulder and give it a small squeeze. "I think something like that probably never leaves you."

"Yeah, I guess. You know, I've never told anyone that before." He scrubs his hand down his face and I let my hand drop from his shoulder.

"Your secrets are safe with me."

He turns his head and meets my eyes. "I know. That's probably why I'm so comfortable talking to you."

Some brief and unnamed emotion passes between us, and I look away and step back as if I'll get burned if I get too close. "We should finish up."

He clears his throat. "Yeah."

Thankfully, there are no more confessions during our session; otherwise, my heart might have started opening for Lee again, and that would be a complete disaster.

twenty-one

. . .

Lee

Another week passes and the team loses to Carolina. I'm more desperate than ever to get back to QB1, but on the other hand, I love the one-on-one time I'm spending with Shayna.

Ever so slowly, her guard is coming down and she's opening up to me. Maybe not as much as she did in college—she still pulls away sometimes when she thinks we're getting too close—but we've transitioned to a place where she's not haunted by the past every time she looks at me anymore.

My MRI on Monday showed that things are progressing well and the small tear on my rotator cuff is healed, but my AC joint still isn't completely ready. Which means yet another week I'm stuck on the bench instead of where my team needs me.

"This is so fucking frustrating." I'm bent over, doing one of the exercises Shayna gave me.

"Hey." She bends too so she's at my eye level. "Progress is progress. You're almost there. You just need to be patient and keep putting in the work. The payoff will come."

"I'm so sick of everyone telling me to be patient. I've been fucking patient."

She straightens and sets her hands on her hips. "You need to stop whining. Your rotator cuff is fine. You have full range of motion back in your shoulder. Now we just need to let it heal some more while we work on increasing the load the joint can take without reinjuring it."

I straighten up. "All I hear you saying is that I'm going to be useless for yet another week."

"Check the attitude, Lee."

"Wouldn't you have an attitude if you were in my position?" My voice comes out louder than I intend, and her lips thin and the crease between her eyebrows deepens.

"Actually, I think I'd be thankful I didn't need surgery, and that the tear on my rotator cuff was healed, and that I haven't had any setbacks, but hey, that's just me." She throws her arms in the air as though she's totally exasperated with me.

"That's pretty easy to say when you're on the sidelines."

She steps forward, her hands fisted at her sides. "What's that supposed to mean?"

"You don't know what it's like to be the star of the show and disappoint everyone counting on you."

She guffaws. "Of course, because I'm just the lowly therapist, right?"

"I didn't say that."

"But that's what you meant."

My frustration is close to boiling over. "Don't put words in my mouth."

"You know what? It's almost time for today anyway. We're done. Maybe you should ask a different therapist to take over from here on out."

I don't have time to reply before she spins on her heels and rushes out of the room.

"Fuck," I mutter under my breath and push a hand through my hair.

Not a minute passes before I realize that once again, I need to apologize to Shayna. I let loose my frustration on her and she didn't deserve it. She's only been a help, not a hindrance.

I'll give her some time to cool off, then figure out how to apologize for being an asshole—again.

———

Jesus, I haven't been this nervous since I was a teenager about to lose my virginity.

I stand on the other side of Shayna's apartment door with a peace offering in hand. I'm not really sure how she'll react to my apology, or to my showing up at her apartment. After a deep breath, I knock on the door. I wait, shifting in place until I hear someone behind the door and it whips open.

Shayna stands there wearing a matching blue-and-white-striped shorts-and-tank pajama set, bare feet, some kind of fuzzy headband thing, and a bright-pink face mask all over her face. "What are you doing here?"

Man, her nipples are poking out of the thin fabric of her tank top, and her shorts show off her long legs that look so good wrapped around me. "Um… hey. I brought you something." I hold out the hand that's balancing my peace offering.

She takes it. "What is it?"

"The best cheesecake in the world. It's from my favorite bakery downtown."

Shayna gives me the once-over. "I'm surprised you even have a favorite bakery."

I pat my stomach. "I only visit in the off-season, but it's worth it every time I do."

"You still haven't said what you're doing here." I open my mouth to answer, but before I can, she says, "Wait a minute… how did you find out where I live?"

I cringe and push a hand through my hair. "I may have sweet-talked one of the HR girls into giving your address to me." I raise both hands. "I know, but in her defense, I told her it was so I could have a thank-you gift delivered since you've helped me so much with my recovery."

Shayna rolls her eyes and blows out a breath. I kind of like the way she's not self-conscious with the face mask on. It means she is comfortable around me. "What do you want, Lee?"

I push my hands into the back pockets of my jeans. "To apologize—again. I was a total dick. I took out my frustration on you, and you didn't deserve that. You've only been helping me every way you can. I shouldn't have said those things I did, and I'm sorry."

The sound of a cell phone ringing comes from inside her apartment. She looks at me and then behind her.

"Go. I'll wait."

She hesitates, then steps back and opens the door wider. "Just come in."

I follow her inside and close the door. Her apartment's living area is fairly small, with a couch, a chair, and a TV stand. I assume the kitchen must be off to the right because I see some tile flooring, and the bathroom or bedroom must be the door at the end of the short hallway.

It might be small, but it's neat and tidy and decorated in a variety of soft colors—mostly ivory, peach, and yellow. It's definitely a girl's apartment.

I'm trying not to eavesdrop, but it's hard when Shayna is five feet away and I'm the only other person here. I gather it's her aunt she's talking to, but she only carries on the conversation for a minute before she asks if she can return her call later.

"Sorry about that." She sets her phone on her coffee table. "Have a seat." She motions to the sofa, and I sit on the one end.

She sits in the chair. "Listen, I appreciate the apology, Lee,

I do. And I understand how frustrating this entire process must be for you."

I flop back against the couch cushion. "I have a contract to negotiate at the end of the season. You know as well as I do that damaged goods means you have less pull, which means teams see you as worthless, which means less money and fewer guaranteed years."

Her lips press into a thin line, and she tilts her head. "I'm sure you'll still get a lot of money. This wasn't a major injury. Had it been a season-ending injury, it would have been different."

I'm shaking my head before she's even done speaking. "It's not so much about the money as I want to stay here in San Francisco next year. I like the life I've built here. I love the city and I like my teammates—I think we have a real shot at winning it all over the next few years if we stay the course. The last thing I want is to go play somewhere else and have to start over. The sooner I can get back on the field and prove myself, the better."

Her features soften. "The Kingsmen would be crazy to get rid of you. You're their star player."

I shrug. "Yeah, but everyone's star burns out at some point. What if the Kingsmen think this is my first of many injuries to come? What if they want to get rid of me so that they have a budget to grab the new up-and-comers?"

"I'm sure that's not going to happen."

"Maybe. But the sooner I prove I'm completely over this injury, the better."

"And you're going to be. We're going to keep working, and I have no doubt you'll be back on that field soon."

I hope she's right.

God, she looks so beautiful right now. I'm about to tell her that when she stands from the chair. "Can you give me a minute? I need to wash this off my face. It's so tight now I can barely move my lips to talk."

"Oh, yeah. Of course."

She gives me a small smile and heads down the hallway. A few seconds later, I hear the water running in the bathroom.

While I wait for Shayna to return, I realize that I feel better about everything just from venting. From the moment I met her in college, I always felt comfortable with her. When I held so much in, unable to trust people, I was instantly at ease with her. The fact is, I like being around her—in whatever way she'll let me.

"That's better." She comes from down the hall and sits back down, smiling.

She's fresh faced and god, so fucking gorgeous it's a crime. And she's such a good listener and she's super smart and holds herself and others to a high standard.

Before I can stop myself, the words are out of my mouth. "There's another reason I want to stay with the Kingsmen…"

"Oh?" A small line forms between her eyebrows.

I swallow hard. "You."

"Lee…" She turns her head to look away.

I stand, fisting my hair. "I know I shouldn't say that, but it's true. Jesus, I've tried to keep my thoughts from going there, I really have. But I love being around you. And it's hard when I already know how good we are together. Are you really telling me that you never think about what it would be like if we were a couple again?"

She stands from the couch. "Of course I've thought about it. We always had chemistry—that hasn't changed."

I don't even know what my purpose in admitting my feelings to her was. So she'd say she feels the same? Then what? There's nowhere we can go.

I step up to her, and something like satisfaction courses through me when she doesn't pull away. I rest one hand on her bare shoulder, the other on her cheek. "I want you so bad, Shayna. Tell me to leave before we do something stupid."

She opens her mouth to say something, but closes it and draws in a deep breath.

My lips tingle with the need to feel hers on mine. "Tell me to go and we can toe the line, remain cordial and nothing more than colleagues and maybe even friends. I'm begging you, Shayna, because if you don't, I'm going to kiss you."

She licks her bottom lip and I stifle a groan.

"We..." Her hand presses against my chest, but she doesn't put any pressure into pushing me back. Her fingers pluck at the soft fabric of my T-shirt.

"I know." My voice is ragged, my willpower free-falling.

"Bad idea," she says, and I nod, completely agreeing. "For a lot of reasons."

"Tell me to leave." I hold my breath, waiting for her to respond. The elastic pull between us stretches so tautly it's fraying.

Her lips move, and it takes a moment for my brain to make sense of her words. "I can't."

Snap.

All the air leaves my lungs in a rush and I tug her to me. Her hand fists my shirt, and when our lips press together, it's like returning home. I'll never fuck this up again.

twenty-two

. . .

Shayna

This is crazy.

Crazy *good*.

Lee parts my lips, and when his tongue slides against mine, I moan, sinking into him.

It's just like I remember—all-consuming, fiery, and explosive.

We don't take our time. As if every second of our time apart has come to fruition, I arch in his arms. One of his hands is in my hair, directing our kiss, and the other is splayed against my lower back, pushing me into him where his arousal presses into my stomach.

My hard nipples strain against the cotton of my tank top and I can't get enough of the delicious friction pressing them against Lee's hard chest.

Lee's hands glide down my sides and hoist me up by my ass to straddle his waist. The ease with which he does it is a reminder of his strength. I have a fleeting thought about whether this will be harmful to his shoulder, but my concern dissipates like ether when his hips lunge up and his hard length presses into my center. My head falls back and a sigh escapes me.

Lee's lips travel down to my collarbone, his tongue tracing a pattern up to the shell of my ear. "I can't wait to see you come."

Yes, I want that too. So badly right now. I right my head and shake it, meeting his gaze. He takes the couple of steps over to the couch with me in his arms and lays me on the cushions. When he straightens, he stares at me and I shift in place, uncomfortable with the intensity of his gaze.

"Oh come on, you're not reverting back to my little shy pie, are you?" He grins.

Using the nickname he called me back in college when we first met would definitely have caused me strife only a couple of months ago. But I find that I'm no longer dwelling on the wrongs of our past. The nickname makes me feel special. Not that I'd ever admit that to him.

"Just get down here." I stretch my arms and he falls into them, careful to keep his full weight off me. "That's better."

His lips find mine again, and I ease open my legs. He settles between them and gives me just enough of his weight that I feel surrounded by him in the best way.

Lee takes the hem of my tank top, pulling it up over my head. A flash of self-consciousness hits me, but his face fills with an expression of ravenous hunger and I arch for his mouth.

His tongue circles my nipple, and he tugs gently with his teeth. My hips jut up of their own accord. It's as if a cord of pleasure is running directly from my breasts to between my thighs. He sucks as much of my breast into his mouth as he can fit and releases it with a pop before trailing his tongue to my other nipple.

Then he shifts so that he's no longer fully over me, but more lying to my side. His fingers glide under the top of my sleep shorts. He swipes his hand back and forth, dipping his fingers below the elastic waistband while his mouth worships my breasts.

I'm so desperate for him to touch me between the legs that I whine and piston up my hips. His low chuckle reverberates in my ear until he decides to put me out of my misery, letting his hand coast down to my mound and slide his fingers between my thighs.

He groans and presses his forehead into the hot skin of my chest, drawing in deep breaths. "You're soaked."

I am, almost embarrassingly so, but I don't care. Right now, I'm solely focused on one thing and that's an orgasm.

His finger gently circles my clit and I suck in a breath. Lee uses his teeth to tease my nipple in the same rhythm he's using with his finger. When he shifts so that his thumb is now pressed against my clit and pushes a finger into me, I cry out and grip the hair at the back of his head.

He adds another finger then another, and I arch off the couch cushion. Lee pulls away from my breast to watch me as his thumb strums a delicious rhythm on my clit and his fingers maneuver in and out of me.

My body is strung tight and I'm a begging mess under his spell. Pleasure rockets through me and I cry out, my back arching off the couch while the sensation spirals through every cell. I collapse back, limp and heavy limbed, thoroughly sated.

Lee watches with rapt attention while I catch my breath. I meet his gaze, and though I know this is the part where reality should catch up with me and I should realize this was a monstrously bad idea, none of those feelings surface. Instead, I only crave more of what we just did, more time with him, more *us*.

But is that what he wants? It's not what he said. All his words and his actions have been about the two of us being together sexually, not in a relationship—as though that would even be possible with the issue of the Kingsmen.

All good thoughts for another time.

I wrap my arms around his neck and pull him down over me. "Your turn."

I shift to get up, but he stops me, shaking his head. "I want this to just be about you tonight."

I push forward with my hips a little. "But you must be uncomfortable." My hand trails down his chest, but Lee grabs my wrist before I reach the bulge tenting his pants.

"It's nothing new. I've sort of been in this state since you joined the team." He brings my hand to his lips and kisses the back of it.

I chuckle. "Is that right?"

He nods. "Yeah, and though I love what we just did, I don't want you thinking that's why I came here tonight."

Clearly we're about to have a serious post-fucking-around conversation. "Can I put my shirt on? It feels weird to have this talk with you fully clothed and me shirtless."

He grins. "I like you shirtless." His gaze dips to my chest and he kisses my nipple.

"I'm aware." I push him up by the shoulders and he stands, adjusting himself in his pants. Once my shirt is back on, I say, "Better."

"If you say so." He sits on the couch and takes my hand. "I'm serious when I said that I didn't come here thinking this would happen."

I nod. "I believe you. But now what do we do?"

A small part of me hopes he'll say the responsible thing, which is that this can never happen again. But a bigger part of me wants him to add me to his calendar every night for more of this. We may not be able to have a relationship, but maybe we can have something else… at least for a little while.

He blows out a breath, pushing a hand through his hair in a way that musses it perfectly. "Guess that depends on you. I mean… I want to do more of this, but I get that it's risky. No one from the organization could know that we're fooling around."

Okay, he said fooling around. At least we're on the same page there.

"Agreed."

He arches an eyebrow. "Agreed that it's foolish or that you want to keep fooling around?"

I smile. "That if we *did* keep fooling around, no one could know."

"Okay, and do you want to? Keep fooling around?" He doesn't say anything, and I don't fill the silence. "Not to tempt you or anything, but I held back. I still have some of my patented moves to show you."

I can't fight my growing smile. "Well, I'd be remiss if I didn't give you the opportunity to show me what you're made of, wouldn't I?"

"Completely irresponsible." He holds my gaze and leans closer.

"I guess it's decided then."

"I suppose it is."

"We should probably seal it with a kiss." I smirk.

"You always were the smarter of the two of us." He leans all the way in and presses his lips to mine.

Our kiss lasts a couple of minutes before I pull away. "If you don't leave now, there's a good chance we're both going to end up naked."

He looks as though he wants to say something but doesn't. He stands. "You're right. And just to prove that's not why I came here, I am going to leave." Lee walks over to the door.

I meet him by the door. "I guess I'll see you at therapy tomorrow then."

"That you will." He places a chaste kiss on my lips and leaves.

I stand there for a good few minutes, replaying everything that just happened over and over. I can't believe it. I can't believe it happened or that I let it happen. My only excuse for going along with it is that I wasn't prepared. I hadn't shored up my defenses the same way I do before I show up at work every day.

But now that it's happened, I have to be careful not to fall for him again. It's one thing to let Lee Burrows back into my body. It would be another entirely to let him back into my heart.

twenty-three

. . .

Lee

The entire morning, I've felt like an excited and anxious teenager eager to see his crush at school.

I always look forward to seeing Shayna, but today, it's as though every minute passes at a snail's pace. Though I usually enjoy watching tape and bantering with the guys, today I'm wishing it away because they're all standing between Shayna and me.

Finally, the team heads out onto the field to practice and I go to the rehab room to meet the woman occupying every one of my brain cells.

"Morning."

She looks up from where she's placing some weights and tension bands on the floor and gives me a knowing look. "Morning. How's the arm today?"

I roll my shoulder a bit. "Feels good. Gave my arm a little extra exercise last night and I think it did it some good."

Shayna's cheeks pinken and I smirk. Just the reaction I was looking for.

"As long as you don't overdo it, you should be fine."

I glance over my shoulder to double-check that we're alone, then I walk over to her and place my hands on her hips. "I can't stop thinking about last night." My dick twitches in my pants because the expression on Shayna's face when I made her come last night has been playing on repeat.

"Not here." She takes my wrists and pushes me away, taking a step back.

"We're alone."

She tilts her head at me in a way that says I'm being naive. "Not really though. If we're going to do this, we have to be smart about it."

I adjust myself in my athletic shorts with a cringe. "Fine. But you better believe I'll be making up for it tonight." Now Shayna's cringing. "What? What's that look about?"

"I have plans with Bryce tonight."

My head falls back with a groan. "Are you serious? Can't you get out of them?"

She shakes her head. "Sorry."

"But the next day we're traveling to Atlanta before Sunday's game." Spending any time with Shayna while we're gone will be almost impossible—too many people around.

She sticks out her bottom lip in a pout. "It will have to be after we return home then."

"You're killing me here, shy pie."

She taps me on the end of the nose. "You're a disciplined guy. You can do it."

"It's not like eating my vegetables," I grumble, hands on my hips.

"You're incorrigible."

I groan. "I guess I have no choice."

"Pretty much. Now, should we get started? Don't you dare sulk. I'll make sure to make up for the wait."

That perks me up somewhat. Actually a whole lot. I spend the rest of our rehab session imagining all the ways Shayna might fulfill her promise.

———

The anticipation isn't the same the night before a game when I'm not playing. Sure, I'm still kind of keyed up, but I'm missing that mix of nerves, excitement, and competitive juices.

With any luck, this will be the last game I have to sit out. My shoulder feels as good as it ever has, in no small part thanks to Shayna, and I'm hoping the tests on Monday will show as much.

I flick through a few channels and toss the remote on the bed when I come across *The Blind Side*. Love this movie.

A few minutes later, there's a knock at the door. I sit up in bed, my forehead wrinkled. I have no idea who that could be. It's past curfew, and everyone is supposed to be in their rooms by now. I walk over to the door and look out of the peephole.

It's Shayna.

Elation wars with concern. Is everything okay? Did anyone see her?

I unlock the door and open it quickly, ushering her in. "What's going on?"

It's then I realize she's dressed in one of the fluffy hotel bathrobes.

"Hey." Her smile is mischievous and her aqua eyes sparkle. I'm really hoping that waiting thing is over.

"Is everything okay?" I give her the once-over. She looks fine.

She flips the ice bucket into the chair next to the table. Then she fiddles with the tie on the robe and it slips open, the two sides of the robe falling to her sides. She pushes it off her shoulders and lets it fall to the floor. I expected to find her naked, but it's even better. Shayna's wearing a Kingsmen jersey, and when she spins around, it's my last name and number across the back.

"Fuck, that's hot, shy pie."

She wiggles her ass a bit—which I can't see because of the

oversized jersey she's wearing—and looks at me over her shoulder. "I thought you'd like."

"Love. I fucking love it." I come up behind her and let my hands slide down to her hips, then press my growing erection into her back. "But what were you going to do if someone saw you?"

She spins in my arms. "I was going to lie about locking myself out of my room accidentally when I went down to the ice machine. It's on your floor, you know."

"I told you you're smarter than me." I bring my lips to hers.

We sink into the kiss and I take my time. It's only been days, but it feels like years since I kissed her.

She pulls away too soon. "And I told you that I'd make up for the fact that we couldn't see each other for a few days."

"You're a woman of your word."

Her hands slide down my bare chest until she cups my hard cock and squeezes. "Am I ever."

Shayna drops to her knees in front of me and my breath sticks in my throat.

"What are you doing?" I whisper.

"Living up to my word." Her lips press against the fabric of my black boxer briefs and my straining erection.

"You don't have to."

"I want to." She gives me a look that makes me think this woman was made for sin, then she eases my boxer briefs down my legs.

When the fabric drops to my ankles, I kick them out of the way. Shayna fists the base of my cock with one hand and gently runs her mouth up and down my shaft. But she doesn't open her mouth or give me her tongue, something that makes me needy and causes my dick to twitch in her hand.

"Patience, patience," she teases.

Her hot breath hits my sensitive skin and when she

squeezes the base a low growl sounds in my throat. She must take it as a sign that my patience is about to snap because this time when she drags her mouth from base to tip her tongue drags along with it.

I groan when she sucks the tip into her warm, wet mouth, and my hand goes into her hair, but I restrain myself from forcing her to do what I want, letting her remain in control. Shayna slides her mouth down my shaft. When she retreats back to the tip, her hand follows, squeezing that perfect amount.

She repeats the motion over and over. My hand tightens in her hair, and she moans around my cock. Fuck, the sight of her plump lips wrapped around my cock, wearing just my jersey, takes me to the edge too quickly. When her other hand gently squeezes my balls, I can't hold back any longer.

My hips move on their own and she lets me take control. I fuck her face while her expressive eyes stare up at me, and that's when I decide that I want to see myself on her, like a branding.

"Lose the jersey." My voice is commanding.

She wastes no time, pulling the jersey up and over her head, then her mouth is back on my cock again. I push my hand in her hair and don't hold back. I love the way her tits bounce every time I bottom out at the back of her throat. Before long, my balls tighten and I'm on the verge of coming.

I pull out just in time to jerk myself off onto her tits, groaning while I paint her milky skin white. My softening cock twitches in my hand when she drags a finger through my cum and circles her nipple.

This woman could very well be my undoing.

"Hang on a second." With shaky legs, I walk into the bathroom, wet a washcloth under warm water, and bring it back to her.

She holds out her hand to take it from me, but I'm nothing if not a gentleman. I get down on my knees in front of her and wipe my cum from her chest. When I'm done, I toss the wash-cloth to the side.

"Best surprise ever." I take her in my arms, showing her with a kiss just how much I enjoyed what we did.

"Glad you think so." She pulls back and stands, grabbing the jersey and pulling it over her head.

"Can I get a picture of you wearing just that? I want to memorialize this moment." That's code for "I want to jerk off to it for months."

She worries her bottom lip. "I don't know, what if someone sees it?"

"I would never show anyone."

"All right." She poses for me.

I snap a picture, clicking the little heart so it will appear in my favorites folder on my phone.

When I'm done, she grabs her robe off the floor and slides it back on. "I'd better get back to my room. We have an early start."

"Stay. I can pay you back." The disappointment that flares in my chest is a surprise even to me. I wish she could stay the night, but it's risky.

"If only. Only a couple more days." She makes her way to the door and gets up on her tiptoes to look out the hole into the hall. "All clear." She turns around to face me. "I'll see you tomorrow."

"All right." The words "thank you" almost leave my lips, but that would be weird, right? "Counting down the seconds."

She smiles then opens the door and darts out into the hall. I lock the door behind her and go to lie back on the bed.

Though I'm more relaxed than I have been all week, it takes a while for me to drift off to sleep because I can't get Shayna out of my head.

twenty-four

· · ·

Shayna

"Woo-hoo!"

The celebratory sound comes from the doorway of the rehab room. Lee sprints across the room with a contagious smile, arms wide open. He lifts me by the waist and spins me around.

I smack his shoulders. "Put me down. My god. What are you thinking?" I push at his hands on my waist and he sets me on the ground.

"I'm cleared to play!"

I'm not sure I've ever seen Lee this happy, and it's so great to see after the hard work he put in. I want to hug him and kiss him and praise him, but there are too many prying eyes. "Congrats!"

"It's all because of you." He reaches for me, but his hand drops.

I wave off this comment. "You did all the work."

Truthfully, Lee is the hardest-working athlete I've ever worked with. He had his moments of moping around and feeling sorry for himself, but they were few and far between. It's clear that once he sets his mind on a goal, he'll do whatever it takes to achieve it.

"Well, you can be very motivating." His words drip with innuendo.

"Is that so?"

"I'm not interrupting anything, am I?"

I startle when Dr. Carlisle walks into the room. "Not at all. Lee was just telling me the good news."

He looks between us for a beat. "Yes, he insisted on being the one to tell you."

I shift in place. "I guess we were both working toward the same goal…"

"Yeah, because it's all due to her. She got me back on the field," Lee says, staring at me a little too adoringly.

I smile, trying to convey to Lee to cut it back a little. I don't know if I'm being paranoid or if Dr. Carlisle is staring between the two of us like his lunch was stolen from the break room fridge and we have tuna fish breath.

"Since our work is done, I'll go join everyone else at practice." I gesture toward the door.

Dr. Carlisle gives me a small smile. "Good work, Shayna."

My shoulders relax. "Thank you."

I rush out toward the practice field. My phone buzzes in my back pocket when I'm halfway there.

Lee: *I want to celebrate tonight. You free to come to my place for dinner?*

My steps slow as I take in his words. Dinner? That sounds like a date.

As if he can read my mind, another text comes through.

Lee: *Not like a date or anything. Just a way for me to say thank you. And maybe a little sex for dessert.*

I chuckle and guiltily scan the immediate area, more paranoid due to Dr. Carlisle's accusatory eyes on us moments ago.

Me: *Sure, what time?*

Lee: *Say 7pm*

Me: *See you then.*

Holy shit, I'm going to have sex with Lee Burrows tonight. New panties and bra, shave and lotion up, wax, shit I need to get a wax job!

But I can't think about that right now. Right now, I need to focus on my job, because if I start thinking about Lee and all the things we might do to each other tonight, there's a pretty good chance my blush will give me away. No one on the Kingsmen can know that I'm sleeping with their starting quarterback.

———

I arrive at Lee's a couple of minutes before seven, feeling as if I'm on some kind of spy mission. I felt as if every person I passed along the sidewalk toward Lee's building knew where I was going and what I was going to do. And then once I was in Lee's building and past the concierge, it felt as if the handful of people in the elevator with me were giving me judgmental looks.

Talk about paranoid—I even looked over my shoulder after each step.

I know it's all in my head, but I didn't realize that sneaking around would be this stressful.

Lee's waiting for me when the elevator doors open. He's dressed in dark denim and a button-down maroon shirt. It's untucked and the sleeves are rolled up to reveal his strong forearms.

I opted for dark denim also, but I have on a red shirt and black pumps.

"Hey, shy pie. You look great."

He wastes no time anchoring me to him with one arm around my waist and his other hand brushing away my stray hair, locking his lips to mine. He smells fantastic and tastes even better. Our kiss turns into a hug and I inhale his cologne, wanting to embed this moment into my memory forever.

Lee's hands slide up and down my back until he pulls away. "If we keep that up, we won't get to dinner."

I give him a cheeky smile and trail my finger down his chest. "I don't mind skipping dinner."

It's true. All I thought about today was rolling around naked with Lee all night.

He chuckles and leads me into his condo toward the kitchen, his hand in mine.

"It smells fantastic in here." I glance around the kitchen and see a frying pan on the professional range and a cutting board. Somehow I thought he would have ordered takeout. "Did you make dinner yourself?"

I step over to the stove to see a mixture of thin slices of meat along with vegetables and pasta in a frying pan.

"Why do you sound so surprised?" He opens one of the cupboards and sets two plates on the counter.

"I figured you'd probably have food brought in or maybe a chef. It's unusual for the league's top quarterback and bachelor to also know how to cook."

He shakes his head playfully. "Always underestimating me." Lee uses the spatula to dish the meal onto the two plates. "Truth is, when I was growing up, either I cooked or starved." He shrugs. "And bowls of cereal and Ramen noodles didn't do it for me when I was a growing teenage boy." He winks, playing off his childhood.

There's a pang in my chest when I imagine a teenage Lee left to fend for himself.

"Well, it smells incredible. Can I do anything to help?"

"Pork and pepper pasta. One of my faves." He nods

toward the island where a bottle of wine is already uncorked. "Do you mind carrying that into the dining room?"

"Can do." I pick up the bottle and follow him to the dining room where he sets the plates down across from each other.

I sit in the closest chair, and Lee sits directly across from me.

"Wine?" He lifts the open bottle near my wineglass, and I nod. He pours for me then pours himself a glass. He sits back down and lifts his glass. "I'd like to make a toast."

I lift my glass.

"To you, for helping me reach my full potential again."

I clink my glass with his. "To us, because we each had our part to play."

He smiles. "We do make a good team."

I should let that comment go, although I agree, so I bring my glass to my lips and sip. "That's good wine."

"Let me know what you think of the meal."

I pick up my fork and stab a piece of pasta and pork. Lee watches while I chew, waiting for my reaction. Flavors burst on my tongue and I make a "mmm" sound.

"Oh my gosh, that's so good," I say when I'm done chewing and swallowing.

Relief fills his eyes, and it warms my heart that he is concerned about my reaction.

"So is this the dish you break out when you want to impress one of your dates?" I spear another piece of pasta, then realize how what I said sounds. "Not that this is a date or you want to impress me."

He chuckles. "No need for the disclaimer. Actually, I've never made this for anyone except my mom and my brother."

"Really?" I reach for my wineglass.

"Really. Don't you know by now?"

I lose myself in his hazel eyes.

"You're special, shy pie." He winks.

I hate the thrill that rushes through me at his words. "Careful, all this praise might go to my head."

"Wouldn't be the worst thing in the world. You still have no idea how fucking amazing you are, Shayna."

My cheeks heat and I look at my plate. If this were a regular... relationship... I'd bask in the warm glow of his comments, but it's not. I'm here for physical pleasure and to get him out of my system. I cannot afford to fall for this man.

I meet his gaze. "Lee, you can't say things like that. That's not what this is."

His shoulders slump and he sets down his knife and fork. "You're right. I'm sorry. But you can't blame me if you're my favorite person in the moment. You helped me get back on the field."

I laugh. I guess he's viewing me as the reason he got what he wanted even though in truth, it was him. But he's on a high and I'm not going to ruin tonight by putting disclaimer stickers on every comment. "All right. You're forgiven."

We eat in silence until I can't take the awkwardness any longer.

I ask the first thing that comes to my head. "Are you close with your brother?"

He finishes chewing. "Yeah, we're pretty close. Honestly, that didn't come until we were both out of my parents' house and away from our mom."

My head tilts. "How come?"

Lee shrugs. "We don't have the typical brotherly relationship since he had to take me under his wing after my dad died and my mom checked out. In a lot of ways, he was like a father to me. Plus, he was always kinda shut down emotionally. But all that's changed now."

"Because he's married?" Just google either Lee or Kane Burrows and you'll see Kane Burrows married Jana Gerhardt, the heir to the Florida Fury. I wonder how their relationship was viewed. The coach and the owner getting married.

Lee nods. "Yeah, Jana really brings out the best in him and I feel closer to him now that he's not hell-bent on telling me how not to live." He rolls his eyes at his brother's expense.

"And your mom? Do you talk to her?"

Tension coils in his shoulders.

"I'm sorry. We don't have to talk about her if you don't want to."

He puts down his fork and wipes his mouth. "It's fine." After a long sigh, he continues. "I talk to her here and there, but we're not close. My aunt keeps an eye on her, but honestly, it's usually just a cycle where she'll be doing well, then stops taking her meds, then she has a big episode and ends up at the hospital, goes back on her meds… rinse and repeat."

"That must be really difficult."

He glances out the window at his million-dollar view. "It is. Sometimes it feels like it would be easier to not deal with it at all, not check in on her and stuff, but… she's my mother."

I doubt Lee shares information about his mother with anyone. I'm honored he feels he can trust me, so I squeeze his hand.

Peeling back the layers of Lee is only sucking me in further.

twenty-five

. . .

Lee

The way Shayna is looking at me now… God, I'd do just about anything to have her look at me that way for the rest of my life.

I meant what I said earlier—she has no idea how amazing she is. But she's right when she says that's not what this is.

Time for a distraction.

I finish off the remains of my wine before pushing back from the table. "Time for dessert."

"Please tell me it's that cheesecake from your favorite bakery. I swear that was the best cheesecake I've ever eaten." She eyes me funny as I walk around the table to her side.

"Even better, actually." Taking her hand, I pull her up so she's standing in front of me. Then I pick her up by the waist, walk to the far side of the table, and deposit her on the end.

"What are—"

"Did you forget?" I lean in close, my breath tickling her ear. "You're dessert, shy pie."

She groans, and I gently press on her chest so she's lying on the table. I remove her shoes one by one and set them on the floor. When I run my hands up her jean-clad inner thighs, she gets up on her elbows, watching the hunger in my eyes. I keep my eyes on her, flicking the button and lowering the zipper of her jeans. Fuck me, she's wearing red lace panties. My hands hook on either side of her jeans and she arches up, lifting her ass so I can pull off her pants.

"I see you still like nice lingerie." I arch an eyebrow.

"Problem?" She licks her bottom lip, her chest rising and falling.

I shake my head and continue pulling down her pants. "Fuck no. I used to love knowing that underneath your prim facade, you wore sexy lingerie. I was practically hard all through biology class."

She chuckles when I finally get her jeans off and toss them onto the floor behind me.

I dip my finger under the waistband of her panties. "These will stay on for now. But let's put the heels back on."

She bites her bottom lip. My dick grows excruciatingly hard while I slip her black pumps back on her feet.

"Time to dig in." I fall down on my knees, which puts me at the perfect height to feast on her pussy.

Grabbing her waist, I drag her toward me until she's lined up with the edge of the table. My finger slides down the side of the soaked red lace between her legs and I pull it to the side, showing her in all her glory. She says my name like a prayer.

I take a moment to stare, memorizing her on my dining room table, her pussy glistening with wetness from my hands on her.

She squirms in place. "Lee," she begs.

"Patience. Remember patience?" I chuckle and slowly move her legs over my shoulders.

Leaning closer, I push the red lace aside again and swipe my tongue from her entrance up to her clit. She tastes sweet and earthy and is the perfect aphrodisiac. My cock grows more painful in my jeans. When I lick her again, she moans and jerks her hips, so I use one hand to press down on her abdomen to keep her in place.

I take my time, circling my tongue around her entrance then her clit, alternating the rhythm and pressure I use so that she doesn't come. I look up at her through her spread legs. One of her hands kneads her breast, pinching her nipple, and the other goes into her hair. I swirl my thumb over her clit and fuck her entrance with my tongue.

"Oh god… Lee…"

I love the way my name leaves her lips in such a breathy, desperate way. Maybe it's the athlete in me, but I'll never be done with her needing to feel me the way she is right now. I own this orgasm and she'll leave this condo knowing she'll never get anything like it anywhere else.

I push down a little harder with my thumb and rapid fire my tongue in and out of her. Shayna's back arches off the table. She squirms more and I hold her down on the table. Her heels dig into my back.

"Oh god," she cries out when her orgasm hits her.

Continuing to lap her up, I groan at the taste of her and slowly bring my thumb to a stop until she's wrung out completely.

"Wow." She lies there, panting and staring right at me.

I stand and slide the red lace back over her mound, staring at her with a raging hard-on and a self-satisfied smile.

When her breathing returns to normal, she props herself up on her elbows and looks at me. "A man of many talents."

With a grin, I take her hands and help her into a sitting position. "Oh, baby, that's just a forkful."

She yelps as I pull her up off the table and over my shoulder. My hand squeezes her ass.

"What are you doing? Lee, put me down." She swats my ass while I walk us down the hallway to my bedroom.

We enter my room and I deposit her on my bed. Damn, she looks good there.

"You're insane," she says with a laugh.

"Insane for you."

There's a brief moment when I regret the words. Not because I don't mean them, but because her energy shifts from carefree and playful to something more serious. She's so worried about keeping us on the one side of the line.

So rather than let us veer into some awkward conversation, I shred my shirt and flick the button of my jeans, hoping she'll let it go. I lower my zipper and my cock thanks me for freeing him. The heat in her eyes returns as she watches me strip down.

"Your turn." I crawl over her on the bed and pull her shirt up by the hem until it's over her head.

I'll never forget this vision. Her lying on my bed, looking exquisite in her red lace bra and underwear and black heels. I wasn't lying when I said that I loved being the only one in the room who knew that under her put-together, good-girl exterior was a set of sexy, high-end undergarments. It's like our own little secret—as if we don't already have a bigger secret that we're keeping from everyone.

"You're stunning." I drag my tongue down the center of her chest and over the red lace. I tongue her nipple through the thin fabric before tugging on the sensitive bud with my teeth.

Shayna's hands dive into my hair, so I repeat the motion with her other nipple. She writhes underneath me as my cock grows harder by the second. I'd love to tease this out for her longer, but there will be plenty of time for that later. Right now, I need to be inside her.

I press the fastener in the middle of her breasts and the bra pops open. Taking my time, I peel back the lace until she's bared to me. Sucking in a breath, I cup each breast before swirling my tongue around each nipple. She sighs and tightens her grip on my hair.

I sit back and slide the underwear down her legs, then

remove her heels. I can't help but take a moment to soak her in as I get off the mattress and slowly pull down my boxer briefs. I stand over her, stroking myself as I admire this woman laid out before me.

"You really are built like a god, aren't you?" Shayna says, her arms stretched for me to come to her.

I chuckle. "You're saying that like it's a bad thing." I kneel on the edge of the mattress.

"Not bad per se, but how are any of us women supposed to resist?"

"I'm only worried about one woman." I crawl up the bed over her, the head of my cock dragging over her skin until our waists are aligned. Shayna arches up so that her nipples brush my chest, and I groan.

"What about birth control?"

Jesus, she's right. I almost forgot myself. Usually it's the first thing I think about before my dick comes even close to a woman's pussy, and I wouldn't even consider sleeping with a woman without a condom, no matter what assurances she gave me, but I decide to be honest.

"I don't want anything between us. I'm clean. I was tested at the beginning of the season, and I haven't been with anyone since."

Surprise flickers in her eyes, but her response doesn't give anything away. "I'm on the pill, and I'm also clean. It's been a while since I've been with anyone."

I'd love to dig into exactly what that means, but the thought of her with anyone else makes me feel possessive beyond control, so I'm better to let that topic go.

"How do you feel about not using a condom then?" I wonder for a moment whether I'm losing it, but those words feel right.

"I'm surprised you'd even consider it." She studies my face for a beat.

"Normally I wouldn't. I've never slept with a woman

without one, but… I know you're not the kind of person who would ever trap me." I want to expand on my statement, tell her she's the best woman I've ever known, the most up front and honest person, but I sense that she'll pull away if I do so.

"Never, Lee. Never."

I smile at her then widen her legs with my thigh before setting my hips over hers. "So you're okay with it then?" I press the head of my cock to nudge against her mound and her eyelids droop.

She nods slowly. "Completely okay."

Reaching down, I drag the head of my cock through her folds, groaning at the feel of her heat and wetness against my hardness. I continue teasing her until she wraps her arms around my neck, dragging my lips to hers.

"God, you're an asshole," she says against my lips.

My chuckle morphs into a groan as I push inside her. She's fucking heaven. It doesn't take more than a few seconds of being inside her tightness before I know I'm thoroughly fucked. No woman has ever felt better and something tells me no woman ever will.

twenty-six

. . .

Shayna

Lee's big and stretches me to a glorious ache. Every nerve ending in my body is lit up like the Golden Gate Bridge at night.

I nip his bottom lip as he slides out of me, thrusting back inside while my hands drift down his back and settle on his muscled ass. Every time he thrusts inside me and his ass cheeks clench, I moan.

The pace starts off slow, building my orgasm slowly, but Lee picks up the rhythm until he's slamming in and out of me. My tits jiggle against his chest with every thrust, providing me with the most delicious friction. I lose myself until I'm so close to coming, I can't clench any harder to keep my orgasm at bay.

But having a professional athlete in your bed means one thing—stamina.

Lee pulls all the way out, and a small whine sounds in my throat. Without a word, he takes my hips and rolls me over so I'm on my stomach, then he pulls my hips up to raise my ass in the air. He sinks his long length back into me with a growl.

"Fuck, Shayna, this view alone. With how fucking good you feel."

I'm right there with him. He's so deep inside me as he drags his cock in and out of me. My fingertips dig into the bedspread, while his dig into my hips, pulling me on and off his dick.

We fuck like two animals, in a frenzy and unable to get enough. Eventually one of his hands drags up my back and around my neck, which he clasps. Not enough to hurt or to block my airway, but with just enough pressure that it feels possessive and I grow wetter.

He pulls me up with the hand around my neck so my back is pressed against his chest. He snakes his other hand around to my front and plays with my clit.

Game over.

"Oh Lee… Lee… Lee…" I repeat his name as he strums between my legs like a maestro.

With one last thrust up into me, I come on a shout. I lose all sense of myself. I fall apart and am put back together at the same time. My hips jerk and everything inside me clenches.

Lee pushes me forward so my cheek is pressed against the mattress and his hand is in my hair at the back of my head. He drags his thick cock in and out of me with a fierce determination. He shatters on a groan, holding himself inside me until he's bottomed out and I've milked him dry.

Neither of us moves, and the sound of our heavy breathing is the only noise in the room.

Lee rolls off me onto his back and drags me into his arms. "That was even better than I remember." His voice sounds somewhat wistful.

"Agreed." It's all I can say—I feel as if my world has been shaken and thoughts are slow to form in my brain.

He kisses my forehead and extracts himself from our embrace, rolling off the bed. "Let me get something to clean you up."

I watch his naked stride to the en suite, admiring the

perfection of his ass. I swear that thing was made to be appreciated.

He returns a minute later with a wet washcloth and holds it out to me. I take it, clean myself up, then excuse myself to use his bathroom. After I've peed and washed my hands, I head back to the bedroom, getting my first real look at his room since I was distracted when he brought me in here.

The room is spacious with dark-gray walls and dark wood furniture. There's colorful abstract art on the walls and very little in the way of personal belongings, though I do spot a framed picture of two boys on his dresser. I assume that's him and his older brother Kane.

Lee rests under the silky gray sheet in the middle of the king-size bed. He has the TV mounted on the wall turned on to the sports channel.

"Come join me." He pats the spot beside him.

That's when I realize I'm standing here buck naked. Sliding under those covers is more relationship status than just screwing one another.

"I should probably get going." I walk over to the bed to pick up my clothes.

He frowns. "Do you really need to leave now?"

In truth, no. It's not that late. I could certainly stay for a couple more hours. But this thing between us is supposed to be just sex, and if I stay, it will feel even more like the line between this being a hookup and something more is blurring.

Still, I don't want to race out of here. I enjoy being around Lee. He's funny, and he makes me laugh. Around him, I'm a version of myself that I don't get to be very often.

"I should probably go." I motion toward the door with my thumb and slide on my underwear.

"No, you should get in this bed with me and chill out." He looks at the television screen. "It's not late."

I bite my bottom lip for a moment, unsure what to do. Lee comes out from under the covers and grabs my hand. I let him drag me onto the bed, then he pulls down the covers and waits for me to slide underneath before he pulls me into his chest and flips through the channels.

I let out a deep breath and relax into him. I shouldn't still be here, but it feels so right at the same time. It's only a big deal if we make it one. Right?

———

I turn off my hair dryer and notice the sound of trickling water, which is weird because I finished my shower fifteen minutes ago. Staring at myself, I tilt my head and listen harder.

Yep, definitely hearing something.

When I open the bathroom door, the sound is louder. I follow it through the living room into the kitchen, where water trickles out from the cabinet underneath my sink.

"What the hell?" I rush over and hunch down, pulling open the cabinet door only to be sprayed in the face with water. "Oh my god!"

I push the door closed and rush back to the bathroom to grab my phone off the bathroom counter, immediately pulling up the superintendent's number to call him. I hit speaker on my phone and rush to the linen closet in the hallway, grab a bunch of towels, and rush back to the kitchen.

When the super's voice mail comes on, I curse and leave him an urgent message. "Arthur, it's Shayna. A pipe or something has burst under my sink, and I don't know what to do. Call me back right away or, better yet, just come over."

I dial his number again, but it goes to voice mail again. I don't bother leaving another message.

Dropping to my knees, I place towels all around to absorb the water that's already on my kitchen floor. I decide that I'm best to leave the cabinet closed and just deal with the water that escapes since I have no idea how to turn the water off in my apartment.

Maybe Google can help me. But first I need to get more towels.

I rush back through the living room to grab more towels from the closet when my phone rings in the pocket of my robe. I answer without looking at the screen.

"Arthur, did you get my message? I need your help!"

"Should I be jealous of Arthur?"

Lee's voice makes my stomach sink. Normally I'd be ecstatic to hear from him, but I really need Arthur to call me back.

"I'm sorry, Lee. I have to go. A pipe just burst in my kitchen and I'm waiting for the superintendent to call me back. And I really need to buy more towels the next time I'm at the store." I don't wait for him to say anything. Instead I hit end on the call, grab more towels, and race back to the kitchen.

The towels I initially put down are soaked at max capacity, so I pick them up and put down new towels, taking the wet ones to my tub to wring out.

I'm going to run out of towels if I don't figure out how to turn off the water. Grabbing my phone from the pocket of my robe, I do a quick Google search. Before I can sort through the results, there's a knock at my apartment door.

Oh, thank god. Arthur must have gotten my message.

I rush over to the door and swing it open. "Arthur, I'm so glad—"

Lee stands on the other side. He doesn't say a word but pushes past me.

"Lee, what are you doing here?"

By the time I come around the corner, he already has the kitchen cabinet door open and is kneeling, being sprayed with water. He doesn't answer my question. Instead he uses one hand to direct the water away from his face and gets into the cabinet up to his shoulder. Thirty seconds later, I hear him grunting. The water slows to a trickle before it eventually stops.

"Oh my god, you did it! Thank you!"

He backs up from inside the cabinet and uses his hand to wipe the water from his face. He's drenched, but so am I, so I rush to him once he's standing and give him a big hug.

"I was around the corner when I called."

I pull away and push some of the wet hair off his forehead. "Thank you. I didn't expect you to drop everything and rush over here."

"I know." He gives me a chaste kiss on the lips. "I'm double-parked in front of your building, so I'd better go before my vehicle is towed." He squeezes my shoulders then brushes past me on his way to leave.

"Wait, what did you call for in the first place?" I follow him.

"I was gonna be early to the training center and I thought… I wonder what Shayna would think of a quickie…" He grins, then opens my apartment door. "But we can figure out the answer to that another day. At least this way the immediate problem has been dealt with."

"Oh… well, thank you."

"See you soon." He winks.

My stomach flips and he's off like Superman.

I stand there for a moment, trying to identify the feeling invading my chest. It feels vaguely familiar, but I'm not sure. After I leave another message for Arthur, letting him know that the water is off, and I've cleaned up the water as best I can, I think I figure out what it is.

This is what it feels like when you can rely on someone and trust them to have your back.

twenty-seven

. . .

Lee

We flew to Atlanta earlier today for our game this weekend. It'll be my first time out on the field since my injury and I'm anxious for Sunday afternoon to come so I can get out there and show everyone there have been no lasting repercussions to my shoulder. Everyone will have their eye on me—all my teammates, the press, and other teams. I have to prove to them all that I'm as good as I ever was—better even.

Tomorrow is the big day, and a bunch of guys from the team and I just went out for dinner and returned to the hotel bar to grab a few drinks before we head to our rooms to make curfew.

I'd rather be between Shayna's legs right now, but I haven't had a moment to speak to her today. It's like now that we're actually sleeping together, she wants to pretend we don't even know each other, which is ridiculous. Everyone knows she's the one who got me back on the field.

"You're in a good mood. You get laid last night?" Brady asks before tipping back his beer.

"He's right. You haven't stopped smiling all night. It's weird," Miles says from beside me.

I shrug. "I'm just happy to be back in the game tomorrow."

"What do you think, Chase?" Brady asks.

"I don't give a fuck if he's getting laid or not as long as he's on that field and ready to play tomorrow." He picks at the label on his beer, watching his alma mater, Alabama, play.

"I will be. No worries there." Miles looks at me for a beat too long, so I decide to say something that will get him off the scent. "What about you guys? Seems to me if you were hooking up, you'd be less concerned about my sex life."

Brady laughs. "Don't worry about me. I do all right."

Miles shakes his head. "That's like saying that Lee can throw a few yards in a game."

Brady shrugs and grins in that way that is half-cocky and yet half-charming. He's the kinda guy who's cocky enough that you want to hate him, but there's something so likable about him at the same time. I have to think women have a hard time hating him the morning after.

"You get us a win tomorrow, Burrows, and you can fuck my sister for all I care." Chase takes a pull off his beer.

"I didn't know you had a sister," I say.

"I don't." He sets his beer back on the table.

"What about you, Miles? That go for your sister too?" Brady asks, laughing before Miles can even answer.

Miles goes still, his beer bottle halfway to his mouth. "Do not joke about fucking my sister."

Chase shifts in his seat, and Brady raises both hands. "You gotta lighten up. I was just joking, man."

As if Miles didn't hear Brady, he continues. "Twyla is off-limits. I already have to deal with the fact that she's engaged to that idiot. I couldn't handle her hooking up with one of my teammates. She deserves better than any of us."

"Hey, I like to think I'm quite the catch," Brady says with mock offense.

"Let's be honest, there will always be holes in your net." Miles arches a brow.

Brady shrugs.

"Way to spoil the mood," I say to Miles.

Miles flips me off by running his middle finger up the bridge of his nose.

My phone buzzes in my pocket and I slide it out to see a text from Shayna.

Shayna: *What room are you in?*

Oh, I like where this is going.

Me: *2102*

Shayna: *I know it's getting late but what do you say we find out the answer to your question?*

I frown at the phone. Does she think she's texting someone else?

Me: *What question?*

Shayna: *Do I like quickies?*

Me: *I'll be there in ten.*

I slide my phone back into my pocket and finish the last of my beer. "I gotta go wind down before bed. Refresh the playbook. Big day tomorrow."

With raised eyebrows, Brady eyes my phone that's stuffed in my pocket.

"Did you just get a booty call?" Miles looks at me skeptically.

"Exactly my thought," Brady says.

"Yeah, the night before one of the biggest games of my life." I push back from the table. "See you guys later."

All three of them laugh as I leave, but I don't think any of them really think I'm on my way up to meet someone. At least I hope so.

———

"Congratulations. You were amazing." Shayna kisses me and walks into my apartment.

We won yesterday's game, and based on what I read online, there's no doubt that I'm back to performing to my full potential. Getting back out there and making my contribution to the team felt so good. Brady and I were on fire. Three touchdowns. It was like if I threw the ball, it was a magnet drawn to his hands.

The only shitty part about yesterday was not being able to celebrate it with Shayna the way I wanted. Instead, she avoided me and would barely look at me on the plane ride back.

"Couldn't have done it without you."

She smiles from over her shoulder and walks into the kitchen to grab herself a water out of the fridge.

I love that she feels at home here.

After she's taken a healthy sip from the bottle, she pulls it away from her mouth. "Sorry, I'm so thirsty from being at the gym."

"No worries. You hungry? I was going to order something in. Thought we could watch a scary movie while we eat."

Halloween is in a couple of weeks, and all the previews of the scary movies made me want to watch one with Shayna. I like the idea of Shayna snuggling up to me because she's scared, but I don't know how she'll take my suggestion. It's not part of the "this is just a hookup" plan.

She pauses then shrugs. "Okay, sounds good. How do you feel about pad Thai?"

"Works for me. Let me pull up the place around the corner." I fish my phone out of my back pocket, and once we've placed the order for the food, we settle on the couch in my living room. "Any preference on what we watch?"

"I haven't seen the new *Halloween* movie yet. Want to watch that?"

"Are you a Michael Myers aficionado?" I punch in the movie in the search function on the TV.

"I've seen practically every horror movie ever made. Scary movies are my jam."

So much for her being scared and jumping in my lap. It will probably be the reverse.

"A sweet, innocent thing like you?" I chuckle.

"You'd be surprised."

"Nah, I've seen you in the bedroom, remember?"

Her cheeks turn deep pink, and she swats me across the chest. "Such a gentleman."

I kiss her, deepening it with my tongue. The kiss gets out of hand quickly, and when I pull away, we're both panting.

"You love that I'm not a complete gentleman," I growl and bite her earlobe.

She laughs and pushes me away. "I'll give you that one."

I pick the movie from the list and it plays. "What's the scariest movie you've ever seen?"

When I settle back into the couch, Shayna leans into me, head on my chest and arm wrapped around my middle. "Ooh, that's a hard one. I don't know if I could pick."

"*The Fourth Kind* is definitely the scariest one I've seen."

She lifts up off my chest to look at me. "I've never heard of it."

"You probably couldn't handle it."

Shayna narrows her eyes, apparently seriously offended

by my statement. "I could absolutely handle it. I've been watching scary movies since I was, like, nine."

"Yeah, I don't think you could." I'm really just razzing her to get her to stay for another movie.

She grins at me. "Challenge accepted. As soon as this one is done, we're watching *The Fourth Kind*."

I shrug. Man, that was easy. "If you insist, but don't say I didn't warn you."

She rolls her eyes and snuggles back into my chest.

"I'm not going to sleep for a week now, thanks. Every time I look out my window, I'm gonna be afraid I'll see a white owl." A full-body shiver racks Shayna's body.

I laugh. "I warned you."

"Sure, but I thought you were just being a wimp or something."

I tackle her so she's sprawled on the couch. "Take it back. You know I'm not a wimp." I tickle her rib cage, and she flails under me.

"Oh my god, stop!"

She can barely catch her breath and I would stop, but I love the look of pure abandon on her face. Her smile could light up this room. Eventually I do stop, but I don't get off her, instead I bend down and kiss her.

"You should stay the night. I hate the thought of you all alone at your place and scared."

"I should, should I?" She stares at me as though she knows I've been playing her all along.

I don't know what I'm doing—tempting fate, I suppose. There have been no sleepovers for us yet. It's been an unspoken rule in order to keep this firmly on the side of hookups only.

But I don't want her to go and I'm man enough to admit

it. What I don't know is whether Shayna is brave enough to stay.

"Okay, I will. But I'll have to leave early to get home and get ready before work."

I attempt to hide how happy it makes me that we're about to teeter the line to something more. "You tell me what time you need me to set the alarm and I will."

"Okay, perfect." She wraps her arms around my neck. "Now, whatever will we do with the rest of our night?"

I sit up and she straddles me, her hot center grinding into the bulge of my pants. "I have some pretty good ideas."

Her hips circle my hardening cock. "You always do."

I bring my lips to hers and we lose ourselves in each other for the rest of the night. I'll never get my fill of her.

twenty-eight

. . .

Shayna

It's Halloween night, and Brady is hosting a Halloween party. I know for certain that most of the players plan to attend, as well as some of the other staff who work on Brady.

I'm bringing Bryce as my plus-one since walking in on Lee's arm isn't an option, something I'm pretending doesn't bother me, but if I'm being honest with myself, I wish we could openly date.

Somehow over the past couple of weeks, our sex-only sessions have morphed into hangouts and sleepovers. I mean, we're still fucking like rabbits too. I'm not sure when the shift happened, but it was an easy transition because I'm so comfortable with Lee—both in and out of the bedroom.

"Have I told you how hot you look?" I say to Bryce as we exit the Uber in front of the address Brady gave us.

"You may have mentioned it." She flips her dark hair over her shoulder. Her jacket is open so I can see the low cut of her leopard bodysuit. "If you can't dress slutty on Halloween without judgment, when can you?" She looks from me up to the house and stops in her tracks. "Holy shit. Brady's loaded."

I take in what is probably at least a fifteen-million-dollar home. "That's for sure."

"Maybe I should rethink being with him. It isn't football money that bought this house."

I don't know enough about real estate to even guess what architectural style his house is, but the property appears to be at least a hundred years old. It's three stories, cream and brown on the outside, and has lots of perfectly manicured landscaping.

"I heard his dad and stepmom are both loaded." I shrug as we make our way up the couple of steps and ring the bell.

The hum of people gallivanting behind the door can be heard, and not a minute passes before Brady swings the door open. He's wearing a *Top Gun* flight suit with a pair of Ray-Bans and I'd be lying if I said it didn't look good on him.

"Hey, you ladies made it. Come on in." He motions us inside where all kinds of people are milling about. Some I recognize and some I don't.

"Great costume," Bryce said, unable to stop herself from flirting.

Brady smooths the front of his jumpsuit with one hand. "Thanks. I'm living out a childhood dream in this one. You want to play the role of tag chaser later, Bryce?" He waggles his eyebrows.

She pats him on the chest. "Sorry, Brady, I'll have to take a rain check on that one."

He laughs good-naturedly and grabs his chest. "Direct hit."

"That's her specialty, isn't it, Bryce?" Miles walks up and joins our group.

Bryce narrows her eyes and scoffs. "Careful, Miles, someone might think you care."

I don't miss the way Miles's eyes zero in on Bryce's cleavage when she removes her jacket.

"That's a great costume too," Brady says, motioning to Bryce.

"Yeah, seems appropriate. Are leopards the ones who hunt or is that lions?" Miles asks.

"Separate corners, you two." I turn to Brady. "Is there somewhere we can put our jackets?"

"Sure, I can take them up to the spare bedroom for you."

I wave him off then take Bryce's. "I can do it. Just tell me where."

He shrugs. "All right. Up the stairs, second door on the right."

I nod. "Why don't you get us some drinks?" I say to Bryce.

"Those you'll find in the kitchen. C'mon, I'll show you the way." Brady shuts the front door and walks in front of Bryce.

The two of them push their way through the crowd as I look at Miles, dressed in his *Anchorman*/Ron Burgundy costume. "Be nice."

He looks as if he wants to say something simpler than what he eventually does. "Fine. I'll try."

I smile and reassuringly pat his shoulder. "Thank you."

Brady's home has old-world charm with extensive wood paneling and a wide wooden staircase past the large grand foyer, but all the furnishings I pass are very modern. It's a nice mix.

I find the spare bedroom, where there's already a massive pile of coats on the bed. That'll make it difficult to find ours at the end of the night, so rather than adding to the pile, I set Bryce's on the chair in the corner and remove my own.

"You wore that costume to drive me crazy, didn't you?"

I whip around at the sound of Lee's voice, and my eyes travel up and down his body. The Zorro costume must have been made just for him.

"Mmm, speaking of…" I walk over, taking a look behind him to make sure no one is in the hallway. "This costume of yours is very sexy. I love the mask. We might have to pull that out in the bedroom."

Lee grins and pulls me into him. "As long as you promise

to wear this for me."

"Deal."

I'm dressed as a sexy referee. All my bits and pieces are covered because I do work with most of the people here, but the entire outfit is made of Lycra and paired with some thigh-high socks and heels. I definitely don't look like the refs these guys see on the field.

Lee groans and dips his chin to press his lips to mine. His hands slide around, lift my dress, and grip my ass, pulling my hips toward him so that I can feel his stiff length at my stomach. Then his lips trail down my neck. "It's going to be impossible to keep my hands off you tonight."

I sigh as he trails his tongue up to my ear. "You have to."

"Maybe we can meet later for a quickie in one of the bathrooms." He punctuates his words by squeezing my ass as he pushes his hips toward me.

"Yeah, may—"

"Where you at, girl? Brady has the high-end stuff, so I made us a—oh." Bryce stands at the doorway to the room.

Lee and I push apart, but I can tell by the way Bryce is looking at me that we haven't fooled her.

"I'm sorry, am I interrupting something?" She cocks a hip and raises an eyebrow.

Damn it.

"'Course not. I just got lost looking for the bathroom." Lee adjusts himself in his pants before turning to face Bryce. "See you ladies later."

He breezes from the room as if nothing happened. Either he thinks she bought his lame excuse, or he's really not bothered that Bryce has caught us.

Bryce steps into the room with a grin. "All right, tell me *everything*."

Guilt settles in my chest that I haven't confessed my sins to what is my one and only friend in California. "If I tell you, do you promise not to say anything?"

One corner of her mouth creeps up in a wider grin. "Of course. I haven't told a soul what you told me about college. You can trust me."

"I mean it. No one can know. Ever. It would be really bad for me."

The salacious look in her eyes morphs to concern. "You have my word."

I take a deep breath and grab her wrist. "Not in here. Someone might come in to leave their jacket."

I lead us to the next room down the hall. It's a little boy's bedroom. This must be Brady's son Theo's room. Once we're inside, I close the door, and Bryce holds one of the two drinks in her hands out to me.

I swallow a hearty sip then blurt it out. "I've been sleeping with Lee Burrows."

"You what?" Bryce leans forward, eyes wide. "Are you serious?" She takes a healthy amount of her own drink. "I thought you were going to tell me he made a pass at you in the bedroom. How long has this been going on?"

I bite my lip. "A while."

"Tell me everything! I want details. Is it as good as you remember or is it better now? Where are you guys meeting up? Have you messed around at the Kingsmen facilities?" When I don't answer immediately, her face drops. "Oh. Oh wait. You're not just *sleeping* with him, you *like* him."

I want to deny it, but I can't. Not to her. Besides, it might feel good to actually talk to someone about how I'm feeling. "It's stupid, I know."

"Hey…" She rubs my upper arm. "It's not stupid. You can't help who your stupid heart falls for."

I set my drink on the dresser and pace the length of the room. "But there's no future for us. It was supposed to just be about hooking up. I thought I could get him out of my system and move on, but the more we're together, the more I want more."

"How does he feel?"

I spin to face her. "No idea. We haven't discussed it because there's nothing to discuss. The rules are very clear—the two of us cannot be in a relationship while we're both members of the Kingsmen organization."

She steps closer to me, a sympathetic look on her face. "Maybe there's some kind of work-around—"

I shake my head. "There's not. I've put myself in an impossible situation."

Bryce frowns. "What are you going to do?"

"Honestly?"

She nods.

"Probably just keep doing what we're doing until it's clear that we can't any longer. It's too good. I don't want to give it up before I have to."

She hugs me with her free hand. "I'm sorry. I wish there was an easy answer for you."

I hug her back and rest my head on her shoulder. "Me too."

We stand like that for a minute before she speaks. "He must be giving you some good *D* though if you're willing to stick around for the heartbreak."

I laugh and pull away. "You have no idea." Just the thought causes my body to heat all over.

"Oh man, I'm so jealous. I'm not getting any good dick from anyone right now."

I take my drink from the dresser and lock our elbows. "Let's go see who's downstairs and see if we can fix that for you, shall we? It'll help keep my mind off a certain quarterback."

"Good luck with that. That Zorro costume is sexy."

"Right?" I laugh and make my way downstairs, determined to make this a fun night even if I know that heartbreak might be around the corner.

twenty-nine

. . .

Lee

The only good thing about Bryce finding out about Shayna and me was that I was able to convince Shayna to head back to my place after the Halloween party, rather than spend the night at Bryce's. Since she didn't have to keep up appearances for her friend, she agreed, and I thanked her by waking her with my face between her legs.

This is a bye week, and since we won our last two games against Kansas City and Los Angeles, we have a few days off the regular schedule.

I plate our omelets, set them on the tray that already has orange juice and coffee on it, and walk it into my bedroom. "Breakfast."

Shayna rolls over to face me, naked under the sheets, with her arms stretched overhead. "Wow. You spoil me." She arranges herself so she's propped up against the headboard with the dark sheet pulled over her chest.

"I aim to please." I walk around the other side of the bed and deposit the tray on her lap, then kiss her forehead.

"This looks great." She beams.

I go back around the bed to my side and slip in under the covers. "I was out of bacon, sorry."

"Can you even eat bacon?" She picks up the glass of orange juice.

"No, the nutritionists at the Kingsmen consider it blasphemy during the season, but you can." I take my plate from the tray.

Shayna chuckles and picks up her cutlery to dig in.

We eat in silence for a minute, but I can tell she wants to say something. The energy wafting off her is far too intense for this time of day.

"What is it?" I ask.

She swallows and sips her orange juice. "What's what?"

"I can hear you thinking from here. What's on your mind?" I spear some egg and bring it to my mouth.

With a sigh, she sets down her cutlery. "We have to be more careful."

I frown. "Would it really be that bad if anyone found out?"

Her head whips in my direction. "Are you serious right now? Of course it would."

"Bryce already knows. What if we just told Miles? He'd never tell anyone. It would give us a little room to breathe if the people we're closest to know."

Shayna shifts a bit so she's facing me more directly. "Lee, Bryce only knows because she found us. We cannot tell anyone else. The more people who know, the more likely that they'll accidentally slip and that would be a disaster."

"I can think of some other words besides disaster." It's hard not to take it personally when the girl you're into says it would be a disaster if anyone ever knew about you two.

She tilts her head. "You know what I mean. There's too much to lose."

My jaw aches with how hard I'm clenching it, trying to keep my thoughts to myself because Shayna clearly doesn't want to hear them. Instead of pushing this conversation now, I'm going to push it to another day.

Her phone rings from the nightstand and she turns to grab it then looks back at me. "It's my mom. Do you mind?"

"Of course not."

"Okay, be quiet though. I don't want her asking questions."

I suppress rolling my eyes and instead mime zipping my lips closed. The obvious panic she has about anyone knowing about us is grating on me. I'm not sure if it's because deep down I want more. I wanted her on my arm at that party last night. I want everyone we come into contact with to know she's mine and only mine.

"Hi, Mom, how are you?" she answers.

She chats with her mom for a few minutes, and from what I gather, they're talking about Thanksgiving. By the time she says goodbye and sets the phone back on the nightstand, I'm finished eating and have set my plate on my nightstand.

"How's your mom?" I ask.

"She's good. Sorry to ask you to be quiet. It's just that we've been playing phone tag all week because she's been working so much. Our schedules haven't aligned, and when you add in the time difference..." She shrugs.

"Where does your mom work?"

Shayna picks her cutlery back up off the serving tray. "Right now, she's working as a waitress at some truckers' diner."

"Oh." I nod.

She turns to face me. "What does oh mean?"

My eyes widen. "It means, oh... like okay."

She doesn't say anything. Instead she stabs a piece of her omelet and brings it to her mouth before chewing aggressively. I didn't even know a person could chew aggressively until this moment.

"Hey, what's with the attitude?" I rub her back.

She sets down her fork and knife with a clatter. "Just your response. Oh. Not everyone can be a big shot, you know."

I raise both hands in a placating gesture. "You know all about my mom. She can't even hold down a job. Who the hell am I to judge? You said, 'Right now she's working at a diner,' which led me to think that there's something behind the right now part and I wasn't sure how to address it, that's all."

She lets a stream of air flow from her mouth and her shoulders sag. "You're right, I'm sorry."

I run my nose up along her cheek, bringing my lips close to her ear. "I swear I wasn't judging her. I'm sorry if it came off that way."

She's shaking her head while I speak. "No, you didn't do anything wrong. This is all me." She sets the tray on the nightstand beside her and turns toward me. "When I was growing up, my mom always had to take odd jobs here and there—the kind most people didn't want... waitress at a dive bar, housekeeping at the local roach motel, fast food, that kind of thing. The minimum wage jobs that didn't require anything but a high school degree."

I take one of her hands because it's obvious that she's uncomfortable talking about this. "Why didn't she ever settle into one job?"

She bites her bottom lip. "When my parents got married, they agreed that my mom would stay home with the kids and help take care of my grandma and my dad would work. Grandma lived with us most of my life because she was sickly. I ended up an only child, but my mom still stayed home and took care of me and Grandma. But when I was around ten, my dad started having problems holding down a job. He hurt his back at work, and that's when the drinking started. He'd go on benders and not show up to work or have poor performance and get fired. Then my mom would be forced to go find a job ASAP to help pay the bills until my dad's phase ended and he found another job. Then she'd be able to stay home again."

I squeeze her hand. "I'm sorry, that must have been hard

to deal with. But I have to say, I think it's amazing that your mom stepped up and did what needed doing to make sure your family was okay. I would have loved to have a mother like that."

She frowns. "That's how I felt, even at the time. I was lucky I had a mom who would take these shitty jobs at a moment's notice so that they could pay the mortgage." She looks down at our joined hands. "My mom is the nicest woman—she'd do anything for anyone. But when the kids at high school would find out where she was working, they'd make fun of me for it. I saw firsthand how people treated her in those jobs too—like she didn't matter, like she was less than them. They acted as if she had nothing to offer, and it broke my heart that my smart, caring, resourceful mother was being treated so shittily."

Tears build in her eyes, and I cup her cheek. "Teenagers are assholes."

"People are assholes," she mutters. "Sometimes I think that's why I've always been so driven to succeed. I didn't want to find myself in the same position as her, and I definitely don't want my kids to someday have to watch me being treated like shit because someone thinks my job is menial."

"There's no such thing as a menial job. People are quick to judge, but if we didn't have people cleaning hotel rooms, or waitressing, or running fast food, or taking away our garbage, or one of a thousand other jobs that make the world run, where would we be?"

She smiles at me. "That's what I think."

"That's what everyone *should* think."

I'm not naive. I'm in a privileged position, but I've never understood people who think they're better than anyone else. Just because I can throw a football doesn't make me any better of a person than anyone else.

"I totally agree." She squeezes my hand.

"How's your dad these days?"

She shrugs. "Better than he was when I was growing up, but he still has his moments. He had back surgery about five years ago that really helped, and my mom says she's seen a real difference since then. But sometimes I feel bad for my mom because there are still so many of my father's debts they must reconcile."

"Why?"

"She never had anyone to trust. No one had her back. She's had my dad's ever since they were married, but due to his addiction, he hasn't had hers. Like she tackled life on her own."

I pull her into me, wishing I could convey to her that she can trust me. I'll always have her back and she doesn't need to be afraid of that with me, but I stop myself because couples just fooling around don't open their chests and promise their sex partner things.

"It sounds like you're heading home for Thanksgiving?"

She nods. "I'm going to fly in and out of Wisconsin. I'll barely be there for more than twenty-four hours, but it's been a while since I've been home. I want to see my mom and my aunt."

"Oh, that sounds like fun."

I set aside my disappointment that she won't be here for Thanksgiving. I'll be staying in San Francisco. It's not Thanksgiving up in Canada, and my brother is busy with the hockey season. Usually I hang out with some of the guys on the team who are still in town.

But this year I had hoped to spend the holiday with Shayna.

She frowns. "I'd invite you but…"

There are so many ways she could finish that sentence—but we're just hooking up, but someone might see us together, but I don't want you to meet my family. I'd rather not hear any of them.

I hold up my hand. "I'll be fine here. Don't worry about me."

She nods. "Can we start this morning over? I feel like I really dragged the mood down with my sob story." Shayna cringes.

I chuckle. "It's not a sob story, it's your life."

She shrugs. "Still." She drops the sheet and I'm distracted by her gorgeous tits as she slides over and straddles me. "We have a few days off. How will we fill our time?"

"Hmm. I can think of a few things." I pull her nipple into my mouth with my teeth.

Her deep sigh echoes in my ears, but so does the sound of a ticking clock. I can't help but feel as though we're on borrowed time.

thirty

. . .

Shayna

I wake on the third day of bye week and know instantly that something is wrong. Even before I open my eyes, the pounding in my head and the cold sweat racking my body are my biggest clues. I squint against the light entering my bedroom through the open blinds. A moan leaves my lips and my limbs are so heavy, just bringing my arm up to cover my eyes is a struggle.

I'm about to drift back to sleep, but there's movement beside me. That's right, Lee stayed last night. We watched a movie and had sex on almost every surface in my apartment. It's completely christened now.

"Are you okay?" Lee's concerned voice asks from over me, but I can't find the strength to open my eyes. The cool press of his palm lands on my forehead. "Jesus, Shayna, you're burning up. Do you have a thermometer?"

"In the bathroom drawer."

His weight shifts off the bed and I hear him rummaging through the drawers in my bathroom. A few minutes later, he comes back into the room. "Found it. You really need to organize your drawers."

I groan. The electronic thermometer beeps and he pushes

it between my lips. I drift off again until the beeping of the thermometer startles me awake.

"Shit. It's a hundred and two. I should call a doctor."

That gets my attention. "No!"

"Shayna, you're really sick."

I crack my eyes open. Lee is sitting on the edge of the bed as if someone just diagnosed me with a serious illness.

"I just need medicine. Something to get rid of the fever."

He nods. "Do you have any?"

I shake my head, but that makes me nauseated. "No."

"I'm going to run to the drugstore. I'll be back."

I mean to say thank you, but my eyelids are heavy and drift shut again.

The next thing I know, Lee is helping me to sit up in my bed.

"What are you doing?" I swat at him.

"Trying to get you to sit up so you can take this medicine and drink a bit. The pharmacist said we need to get your fever down and make sure you get plenty of fluids."

"What's that sound?" I swear I hear the rush of water coming from somewhere. "Did my pipe burst again?"

"I'm running a lukewarm bath. The pharmacist said it will help to bring your temperature down faster."

I'm shaking as he gets me propped up against the headboard. "I'm cold."

"That's just the fever, sweetie." He opens my palm and places pills in it. "Take these. I'll hold the water."

I open my eyes. He's holding a cup of water with a straw, motioning for me to bring the pills to my lips.

"Shayna, if you don't take the pills, I'm going to call the doctor." His tone is annoyingly mean.

I slowly bring the pills to my mouth. Lee presses the straw to my lips. I wrap my lips around the straw and suck back some water until the pills are down.

"All right. I'm going to go check on the water. Be right back."

The water turns off in the tub and Lee undresses me. It feels infantile somehow to let him do this, and I know if I were in my right mind right now, I'd likely be awkward and embarrassed, but I have no will to care.

Once I'm naked, he carries me to my bathroom and gently sets me in the tub. I startle at the water that feels cold against my heated skin. Keeping my head propped up above the water is all I can do though, and I sigh in contentment when Lee holds a cold cloth to my forehead.

After an undetermined length of time, the shivers subside and my head clears.

"How are you feeling?" Lee asks.

"A little better." My voice is weak and hoarse.

"Here." Lee brings a bottle of some red drink to my lips. I turn my head away, but his finger rests under my chin and he directs my face back to him. "It's an electrolyte drink. It's important that you stay hydrated."

Swallowing feels like way too much effort right now, but he's not going to leave it alone, so I take a few mouthfuls.

"I think the medicine must have kicked in and this bath is helping too."

I nod. I'm not one hundred percent, but I definitely feel more human than I did when I first woke. Lee sets the bottle on the floor and stands, bringing the washcloth to the bathroom sink and running it under cold water. Then he comes to sit beside the tub and presses it to my forehead again.

I turn my head away. "Lee, you don't have to do this."

"You're sick. Yes, I do." He says it as if it's a foregone conclusion, but caring for his hookup on her sickbed is not what he signed up for.

"I can take care of myself." I try to put as much steel into my voice as I'm able, but it's a struggle.

He scowls. "I'm not gonna leave you like this."

"You can't afford to get sick." I use the only logical argument I think of that doesn't involve me having to discuss my feelings.

"Then I'll wear a mask, okay?"

I shake my head the little bit I'm able. "There's still a chance you could catch it if you haven't already."

"Jesus, woman, let someone else take care of you for a minute rather than insisting that you do everything yourself." The bite and annoyance in his tone saying he's tired of fighting me.

Tears spring to my eyes because he's right. I'm used to caring for myself. I take pride in the fact that I don't need anyone, but right now, I really don't want to be alone. His presence is a source of comfort, as much as I hate to admit it. "Are you sure?"

"Sweetheart, there's nowhere else I'd rather be." He kisses my forehead, his tone back to loving.

"Fine, but at least get a mask."

He chuckles. "All right. You okay to keep your head above water for a minute? I'm going to go get my phone."

"Yeah, okay."

He's back within a second, his thumbs moving across the screen. "I'm having it all delivered. I'm not leaving you."

I feel defeated to admit that I need him, but I also find I've never been so happy to be defeated in my life.

thirty-one

. . .

Lee

A few days later, Shayna resembles herself again. I end up having to go into the training center a couple of times to watch tape and attend team meetings, but I'm never gone for more than a few hours at a time.

Turns out a few of the medical staff are off ill this week too. Obviously they're passing around a virus, but thankfully, none of the players have been affected.

Coach would cut my balls off if he knew I've been around Shayna in the state she's in and a part of me does feel guilty that I'm risking leaving my team high and dry if I get sick, but there's no way I'm leaving her to fend for herself.

I use the key she gave me for her apartment and push open the door, balancing the smoothie and power bowl I grabbed for her on my way back from the training center. She got her appetite back last night and I'm determined to help her rebuild her strength now that she can stomach eating.

She's in her bedroom, and she's showered and put on fresh clothes. Her color is back and her eyes are no longer the color of a dull pond with too much algae, but their usual Mediterranean hue.

"Someone's feeling better." I walk over to her side of the

bed and kiss her forehead then hold out the smoothie and power bowl.

She picks up the remote and turns down the TV. "I feel like a new woman now that I've showered." She takes the smoothie and sips, then sets the power bowl on the nightstand.

"Good. I got you those to put some nutrition in you."

"Thank you." Her words are somewhat quiet.

"You're welcome." I take off my jacket and set it on the chair in the corner near her closet, then sit on the edge of the bed beside her.

"No, I mean for everything, Lee." Her hand cups my cheek. "You took such good care of me, and you didn't have to. I really appreciate it. I know I'm not the best patient."

"Understatement," I cough out.

She pretends to be upset and I laugh.

"I'm not used to letting people do things for me." Her hand drops from my face, but I pick it back up and kiss each of her knuckles.

"Sometimes it's okay to let people take care of you. Especially those who..." I purposely don't finish and hope she doesn't ask me to. I'm sure she won't, because we've been playing this stupid game like we don't see our relationship evolving.

She nods and sets the smoothie next to the power bowl. "I know that now."

"I'm here for you." I hope she hears the conviction of my words.

One hand grips the front of my shirt and pulls me toward her. Our lips meet, and though I plan to keep the kiss somewhat chaste, she has other ideas. Her tongue glides along the seam of my lips and I open to her, tasting the mint of her toothpaste mixed with the berries from the smoothie.

I push a hand into her hair and deepen the kiss. It's been too many days since I've been able to show my affection for her physically, and it isn't until this moment that I realize how desperate I am for her.

She slowly slides down until she's lying on her back, and I arrange myself over her, spreading her open with a push of my thigh. Our kiss is slow and sensual as if we have all the time in the world. I just want to enjoy her, enjoy us with no rush.

My hand glides over the T-shirt she's wearing, and I thumb her nipple through the fabric. Her hand moves into my hair and tugs in response. My palm slides up and down her body, exploring her over her clothes and showing her we're taking this slow today.

Her soft, warm hands run under the hem of my Henley, tugging until I help her pull it up over my head. Then I do the same, disposing of her T-shirt. My lips trail a path back to her lips and we kiss with our chests pressed together, our hearts beating in sync.

I trail my tongue along her collarbone, casting kisses on her fresh skin until I reach her nipple and pull it into my mouth, swirling my tongue over the turgid peak until she cries out. I make a meal of her other breast, then work my way up back to her lips.

She unbuttons my pants, pushing them down my legs. I get up just to dispose of them and my boxer briefs in one swoop. My socks join the pile of clothes. I stand at the side of the bed, watching her pull down her own pants, leaving her bare for me. She's so gorgeous.

I kneel on the mattress, returning to my spot above her. She welcomes me with outstretched arms. I hover over her and get lost in her eyes.

Neither one of us has to convey that there's something different this time. Before we'd fuck. Sometimes the sex would be hard and fast, other times it would be fun and adventurous. This… this is something different altogether.

There's a weighted feeling to the energy in the room.

We're making love. I've only ever done this once before in my life and it was with her.

I hold her gaze and slowly sink into her depths. My eyes are locked with her aqua ones as I bottom out inside her. A puff of breath leaves her lips and I breathe it in. I want every part of this woman that she'll offer me.

Keeping the pace slow, I glide in and out of her warmth, scanning her face for any sign that she feels the shift the way I do.

When a flash of fear bolts in her eyes, followed by a pooling of water in the corners, I'm reassured she's with me. She is right along with me as we slide over that line of hookup only.

I pick up the pace, unable to continue slowly, our breathing labored. I allow my weight to rest on her and bring my lips to hers, her lips meeting mine first. Our tongues mix in desperation and overwhelming joy.

The tide of pleasure rolls over us and I'm desperate to watch this woman fall over that crest of her orgasm. I slide my hand between us and strum a lazy rhythm against her clit.

She sucks in a breath and her eyebrows arch, creasing the skin at the bridge of her nose. Her plump lips drop open and her back arches off the mattress as she tenses and explodes in waves of pleasure. Her eyes fall closed and a small cry leaves her lips.

After her orgasm has subsided, she wraps her arms around my neck and pulls me into her so my face is pressed against her neck. "Oh, Lee."

I empty myself inside her. An outpouring of love, not just a result of my physical satisfaction.

We lie there pressed against each other, neither of us moving or wanting to pull away.

As I grow soft inside her, I realize the time has come. The two of us can no longer run from the truth.

thirty-two

. . .

Shayna

After Lee comes, I'm quiet for long moments, unsure what to say. I've never felt as connected to someone as I did right then when we made love. I could lie to myself and pretend it wasn't love, but what's the point? There's obviously something different between us, and Lee isn't the type of man who ignores things.

Whereas I'm sometimes content to pretend uncomfortable situations aren't going on around me, Lee is the kind of man who faces them head-on and deals with them out in the open. Maybe in college he wasn't, but he is now.

He rolls off me and, without saying a word, goes into the bathroom. He returns with a wet cloth and passes it to me so that I can clean up. When I finish, he takes the cloth and tosses it in my dirty clothes hamper before sliding back into bed with me.

"So, are we going to pretend?" Lee's voice is low and serious.

I sigh, knowing we would end up here. Because I don't want to have this conversation stark naked, I snag my clothes off the floor and quickly put them on, then I rejoin him in bed.

"I know." God, why do my words sound so downtrodden? I should be ecstatic, shouldn't I? Isn't this what every woman wants? The best quarterback in the league wanting more with her?

"Don't sound so thrilled."

Hurt pools in his eyes, and I take his hand. "It's not that. It's just… that fact brings a lot of real problems along with it."

He nods. "I know, but I'm sick of having to hide away at either my place or yours. Aren't you tired of sneaking around?"

"Of course I am, but what choice do we have? The rules are really clear—you and I cannot have a personal relationship and both work for the Kingsmen."

"Maybe if we go to Giles together and explain the situation—"

"Absolutely not!"

He covers our hands with his free one. "If we explained that we knew each other before you started—"

I drop his hands and stand from the bed. "And what, admit that I kept that fact from the organization during the interview process? Tell them I've been lying for months now to everyone I work with? How exactly do you think that's going to go down?"

He walks over to me and grips my shoulders. "Listen, throwing my weight around isn't something I typically do, but—"

I brush his hands off my shoulders. He's got to be joking. "But what? You're willing to do it for me? I don't want you to, Lee. Even if they did grant us an exception, how do you think I'd be seen by my coworkers or the public?"

He shrugs. "They'd see you as my serious girlfriend, which is exactly what I want… what we both want, right?"

I step into him and cup his cheeks. He's stood on that pedestal a little long and believes not all rules apply to him. "I'd like nothing more than for us to be a couple. To hold your hand down the street and arrive on your arm at parties. Not have to look over my shoulder all the time. But it's not the reality of our situation. Everyone would think of me as a gold digger or the girl who's trying to sleep her way to the top."

He covers my wrists with his hands and brings them down from his face, kissing my knuckles. "But that's not who you are. I know that."

"I know you do. But do you think I'm going to be comfortable going to work every day when all my coworkers are whispering about me?"

He drops my wrist and pushes a hand through his hair with frustration, giving me his back. "So what do we do then? What's the answer?"

I wish I had a good solution, but I don't. The situation is impossible. "Either we keep going along like we are or—"

"Or we stop seeing each other," he finishes.

I nod, frowning.

We stand in silence for a few minutes, neither one of us looking at the other. I'm nauseated by the possibility of things ending with Lee.

Lee looks contemplative, standing with his hands on his hips and staring at the floor until he lifts his chin and makes eye contact with me. "I hate this."

"Me too."

He steps into me and wraps me in his arms. "I can't let you go. I know it's selfish, but now that I have you back, I'm never letting you go." He kisses my cheek.

"I don't want to let you go either."

He runs his hand up and down my back. "We'll figure it out. Let's see what the rest of the season brings." I nod into his chest, then he draws back. "Enough of all this heavy shit. We should be happy. We both just admitted to each other that we want more than sex."

A wan smile crosses my lips. "Yeah, I guess."

"What should we do to celebrate?" He's obviously trying to muster up some enthusiasm.

I play along, trying to ignore the fact this will probably end with a bang.

————

The Kingsmen lose their next game against Los Angeles. Then it's the week before Thanksgiving, so the team prepares for their game against Arizona.

I'm standing on the sidelines, watching the team practice, when Bryce approaches.

"Hey, stranger," she says with a smile.

I chuckle. "We went out for dinner, like, three nights ago."

"I know, but it's so fun to harass you for being a bad friend now that you're getting dicked down by the league's top quarterback."

My eyes widen and I scour the area. Thank God no one is in earshot.

"That's not funny," I whisper-shout.

"Relax, I checked my surroundings before I said anything." She waves off my concern.

"What are you doing here anyway?"

"I'm working on a new piece and I need a few quotes from some of the guys to add to my story."

"Miles on top of that list?"

She rolls her eyes. "I won't even bother asking Mister Sensitive. How's the team looking for Sunday's game?"

I give her a look and she laughs so loudly, a few players turn in our direction. Miles being one of them, but he rolls his eyes and looks away.

"I was just asking. Not like I'm looking for things to print."

"Uh-huh."

"You excited to go home for Thanksgiving?" Bryce changes the subject.

"Yeah…" Lee's name gets called on the field and my eyes zero in on him like always.

"But you wish you could bring your boy too?"

"I do. But I can't stow him away in my luggage."

We share a laugh again. She understands, as I do, that there's no coming out party for Lee and me. In a male-dominated field, there's only a small margin for error when you're a woman.

Bryce swings her arm through mine and nuzzles close, resting her head on my shoulder. "Well, maybe next year."

"Asking for that to be true means one of us doesn't get what we wish for." If we can be seen as a couple next year, it means that one of us no longer works for Kingsmen.

She gives me a sad sort of smile as some of the players come off the field. "I've gotta go to work. Call me later." She walks away but quickly comes back, lowering her voice. "A girl getting QB1 dick shouldn't look so glum."

I shake my head and laugh. "Go. Talk later."

She walks toward some of the players getting water on the sidelines.

"How's that calf?" I ask Chase. He's been complaining about how he got a charley horse the other night and it's still sore and tight.

"Little tight still." He grabs one of the squeeze bottles off the table and squirts water into his mouth.

"Once your equipment is off, come see me and we'll stretch it out while the muscle is still warm."

He nods and walks into the locker room. Lee walks over, sweating, and squirts a stream of water in his mouth. Damn, how did I score this heartthrob of a guy?

"I've got a muscle that's aching," he says, winking.

I widen my eyes then glance around. "Sorry, Lee. Is there something I can help you with?"

"Not at the moment. Maybe later." His smile is so sweet and innocent that a chuckle slips from my mouth.

"Yes, I'm sure you'll think of something—*later*." I hope he'll get the hint and back off.

"Hey, you two." Miles saunters over, helmet in hand, a sweaty mess just like Lee. He leans in close, causing Lee and me to step closer to hear him. "Listen, I don't really know and I don't really care what's going on between you two, other than I'm your best friend." He looks at Lee. "And I haven't betrayed either of you about what happened in the past. That should prove I can be trusted, but whatever," He rolls his eyes. "But people are asking questions about the way you two look at each other. A couple of the guys asked me if you're fucking."

All the air rushes out of my lungs.

Lee is nonplussed. "Fuck whatever anyone else thinks. There's nothing going on."

Miles's eyebrows shoot up. "Yeah well, the press is here, and if they go digging around, it's not gonna take much for them to dig something up. And the more defensive you are"—he sets his gaze on Lee because he definitely gave something away with that reaction—"the further they're going to dig." He looks between the two of us, then glances in Bryce's direction on the field and scowls before looking back to me. "I get that she's your friend, but you can't trust her."

"Lee and I are just friends." My lame excuse comes out halfhearted. Even I hear the lie coming from my lips.

Miles chuckles. "You forget that I was around in college when you guys were eye-fucking each other. Don't worry about me, I figured it out weeks ago. I'm not gonna say anything, but who knows about anyone else." He glances back at some of the guys lingering on the field.

I nod and say a quiet thanks before Miles walks away.

"Why do I feel like my father just scolded me?" Lee shakes his head, watching Miles walk back to the guys.

All I think about is I have to get out of his vicinity. "I have to go. We can talk about this later." I walk away.

"Wait." Lee jogs to catch up to me.

"Later," I whisper over my shoulder.

"Burrows!" Thankfully, the quarterback coach calls him over.

Lee groans, having no choice but to stay on the practice field while I go to do my job.

I hate having to sneak around as much as he does. At first it brought a bolt of adrenaline, but now that real feelings are involved, it's not as much fun. It's not any fun in fact.

But I need to really think this over before I agree to do anything I can't take back.

Lee has to understand.

thirty-three

· · ·

Lee

Shayna gives me the cold shoulder for the rest of the day. I guess I should be used to that, but something about it feels different. Something's *off*. I really wish Miles had come to me first and not involved Shayna.

She does, however, agree to meet me at her place when I text her from the locker room. That's something, I suppose. For a moment there, I thought maybe she was going to tell me we needed to put an end to us.

I'm on my way to my vehicle when I spot Miles heading to his Tesla on the other side of the parking lot.

"Hey, Miles, wait up!" I jog over to where he's waiting for me next to the driver's side. I glance around to make sure no one is nearby. "What the fuck was that earlier?"

He heaves out a heavy sigh. "I'm just trying to help you two."

"By accusing us of having an affair with thirty witnesses and putting the fear of God into us?"

He crosses his arms and leans his back against his car. "Are you?"

We have a stare-off for a moment. I consider lying to him, but what's the point? He already admitted he knows.

"That's not the point."

"That's exactly the *point*."

"You could have pulled me aside privately and talked to me about it. Shayna didn't have to know people were asking you."

"It involves the both of you. Hell, you know what would happen, Lee." He looks over my shoulder, nodding to a player who must be walking to his car.

I look over my shoulder. "Night, Elijah."

Miles pushes off the car and steps toward me. "Listen, I'm just looking out for you. I know you with this girl, remember? You're probably already naming your two kids and the family dog by now. I'm trying to help so it doesn't all go to shit."

I grip the back of my neck with my hand. "All right, thanks, I guess. But next time talk to me in private. You really freaked her out."

He chuckles and grips my shoulder. "Okay, next time you fall in love with one of the athletic trainers on the team, I'll be sure to speak only with you." He shakes his head.

My mouth opens to deny the accusation that I'm in love with Shayna, but I can't deny it. "Thanks, man. You're a good friend."

"Don't mention it." His hand drops and I step back.

"All right, I gotta get over to Shayna's. We need to figure some shit out."

He unlocks his doors. "Good luck. I'll be rooting for you two kids." Sarcasm fills his voice.

I roll my eyes and chuckle, then rush to my vehicle.

The drive over to her place is spent with me thinking of all the arguments I can make to Shayna to let me talk to management about us. We can't go on like this indefinitely. I want to show her off to the world, let everybody know she's mine, not hide in our apartments as though we're doing something wrong.

I knock on her apartment door, and a few seconds later, she answers.

"Hey, shy pie." I step inside and draw her into my arms.

She comes willingly, but there's resistance that's not normally there. It heightens my anxiety.

"We need to talk," she says, pulling away first.

The worst four words in the English language when you're involved with someone.

"I talked to Miles when I was leaving. He was just trying to help."

She nods. "So he knows now too?"

I cringe. "I mean, yeah. I admitted as much, but only because he already knew."

She blows out a breath and paces away from me. "This isn't good."

"It's going to be okay. That's what I wanted to talk to you about."

She stops her pacing and turns to face me. "What?"

"I think we should go to management and come clean."

"We've talked about this. It's a horrible look for me."

"All right, I have to ask." I hold up my hands. "Is this because you don't want things to be more serious between us or is this because of work?"

Disappointment floods every feature on her gorgeous face. "This isn't some excuse because I don't have the balls to tell you I don't want to be more serious with you, Lee. This is about me losing everything I've worked so hard to achieve. This is about everyone around me thinking I tried to sleep my way to the top." She points at her chest.

"That's not going to happen." I grip her shoulders. "Let me handle it."

She shakes her head. "No, let's just wait until the season is over, then we can figure out a plan. The Kingsmen might not even renew my contract for next season—or yours."

My forehead wrinkles. "We're both getting renewed, and

we're going to be together."

She steps away from me and paces again, hands on her hips. "Stop pressuring me, okay? Like I said, we can talk about it once the season is done. See what happens."

I blow out a breath and lean against the arm of her couch. "Aren't you tired of sneaking around like we're doing something wrong?"

She whips around to face me, fire in her eyes. "Of course I'm sick of it. You think I love eating takeout every night or watching movies at home because we can't go out for dinner or to the movies? I'd love to explore the city with you or go hiking on one of the trails. You think this isn't hard on me too?"

"And that's why I want you to let me deal with it. So we can stop hiding and go do all those things together."

"I said no, Lee."

"Shayna—" I step toward her again, but she puts her hand out to stop me.

"Listen, I need to pack to catch my flight home. We can talk about this when I get back."

My chest tightens. "Shayna—"

"No, Lee." She shakes her head. "I just need some time to think about what I want. I'll be back on Friday, but let's wait and plan to talk about it after Sunday's game."

I do my best not to show how hurt I am by her pushing me away. I get the sense that if I push her right now, I'll lose her for good, so I nod and make my way over to the door. "Have a good flight. Just… text me when you land so I know you got there safe, okay?"

She nods, but she's staring at the floor and doesn't look at me.

My stomach churns as I leave her apartment. I refuse to lose Shayna again. I have to do something to make it clear to her how serious I am about the two of us being together. I don't care what it costs me.

thirty-four

. . .

Shayna

I push down on the potatoes with the potato masher, probably harder than necessary. I've been holed up in my parents' kitchen all day under the guise of wanting to help with Thanksgiving dinner, but I'm just trying to avoid all the questions about my life back in San Francisco.

Questions that only spur thoughts of Lee.

I don't know what to do. There's no easy out for us. I meant everything I said to him—I don't want to hide any longer, but I also don't want to lose the job and opportunity I worked so hard for. And what other team would hire me after finding out I got into a relationship with the star quarterback on my previous team? Basically, my life is a mess.

Looking at my mom's and my aunt's situations doesn't help Lee's argument. Two of my favorite women gave up their dreams early in life to be the support their husbands needed, and now they're at the mercy of their husbands.

My mom looks tired and wan from being on her feet all day. Yeah, my dad has been more stable the last few years, but they have mountains of debt to get out from under after all the years when he wasn't doing well.

Then there's my uncle, who hasn't made an appearance

yet at my parents' house. I have no idea if he'll be here for dinner. No one dares ask where he is because we all know the answer is at a bar where he lost track of time or with another woman.

"Why the long face, sweetie? You haven't seemed like yourself since you got home." My mom comes up beside me and rubs my back.

I try to slap on a smile. "Just tired."

"You're working too hard. You need to make sure to take time for yourself."

I scoff. "Like you do?"

She hip checks me and hijacks the potato masher from me. "You're different."

I used to think so, but now I wonder. The thought of throwing away my career so that I can be with Lee stings, but the idea of letting him go is like being swarmed by bees.

"I'm fine, I swear. Just a little run down." I head to the fridge and remove the salad, taking off the plastic wrap, then take it into the living room.

My dad has the football game on and has barely looked away from the screen all afternoon. My aunt sits on the couch with my cousin, Trisha, and the new boyfriend that Trisha brought home to meet her parents. My other two cousins couldn't make it home for the holiday.

Trisha is two years younger than me, and her boyfriend, Scott, seems nice enough. Though if I have to watch the two of them moon all over each other any longer, I'm going to stab myself in the eye with a fork.

Salt, meet wound.

Yet the second reason I've tried to spend the majority of the day in the kitchen.

"Dinner is almost ready," I say, setting the salad on the dining table.

"Sounds good," my dad says without looking away from the TV.

I take everything to the table while my mom carves the turkey, because God forbid my dad be asked to step away from the game. Fifteen minutes later, my mom calls us for dinner.

"Looks great, ladies," my dad says when he sits at the head of the table.

My mom sits at the other end and I'm beside my aunt, across from Trisha and Scott.

"You guys play against Green Bay yet?" my dad asks me once we've all got our plates filled and are ready to eat.

I nod and finish chewing. "Just preseason." Guess my dad doesn't follow the Kingsmen.

"They're looking good this year, even better without Banks."

That's the problem with fans as loyal and crazy as my dad. Brady Banks was praised and worshipped when he played for Green Bay, but because he moved to be closer to his family and probably get more money, they've stripped him to nothing as if he wasn't that great of a player. Even if he's our number-one scoring wide receiver at the Kingsmen.

I cut into a piece of turkey. "They are, but we're doing better in the standings, which has a lot to do with Brady Banks." I'm not sure why I'm purposely going after my dad. I mean, I'm a Green Bay fan too. I mourned Brady Banks when he left the team.

"What's it like working for a professional football team?" Scott asks. "It must be really cool."

I smile and wipe my mouth. "It is. The players work harder than any athletes I've ever worked with, and it's great working with the best equipment and resources out there. There are a lot of cutting-edge treatments coming down the pike, so it's pretty cool to be one of the first ones to get to use them."

Trisha grins at me. "Do you get to massage any of the

players? I swear that team is stacked with hot guys. Especially the quarterback… what's his name?"

I swallow the food in my mouth hard.

"Burrows." My dad groans. "Lee Burrows."

"Yes!" She points at my dad with her fork. "That's him."

"I'm sitting right here," Scott says good-naturedly.

Trisha laughs. "You know you're my number one." She gives him a kiss on the cheek.

I can't help but be envious. Not because she has someone she clearly adores so much, but because she doesn't have to hide it.

"So… do you?" Trisha asks me.

"Trish, leave Shayna alone. She's there to do her job. If there're handsome men around, it's just a perk, right?" My aunt winks at me.

I try to force a natural smile. "Right. The rules are pretty clear about that sort of thing. All the guys and staff are very professional."

A part of me feels bad for outright lying, but for the most part, it's true. It's just not true in one specific instance.

"Boring," Trisha singsongs. "Rules are made to be broken."

Scott looks at Trisha for a long beat before burying his head back in his plate.

Looking to change the subject, I address Scott. "You two didn't tell me how you met."

They look at each other and grin before Scott dives into the story of how his buddy had tried to set him up with Trisha's friend, but Scott knew right away that he wanted to be with my cousin. They look at each other adoringly and share glances that suggest some inside joke between them. With every lovesick glance at one another, the knife twists deeper in my chest.

In any other circumstance, Lee could be here with me. We could be the two fawning over each other in front of everyone, telling the story of how we met. Instead, I'm deciding what's more important to me—my career or the man I love.

The conversation shifts to Trisha's job as an early childhood educator and she relays a few funny stories about some of the kids in her class. We're all laughing over a little boy who brought his mom's vibrator in for show-and-tell because he thought it was a spaceship when there's a brief knock at the front door and my uncle walks in.

Silence falls over the room for a beat before my mom and aunt spur to action.

"Ron, come have a seat beside your daughter. I'll grab another chair from the kitchen," my mom says, pushing away from the table.

"I'll grab you a plate," my aunt says with no emotion and joins my mom in the kitchen.

"Hey, sweetheart." He gives Trisha a kiss on the cheek.

She smiles at him a little warily and introduces Scott.

Uncle Rex smells like a distillery and his hair points in every direction. Even worse, the top three buttons of his shirt are undone and there's a faint stain of pink lipstick on the collar.

My mom brings in the chair. He doesn't bother thanking her or my aunt when she sets a plate and cutlery in front of him.

It's only once he's taken a seat that he even notices me. "Shayna, you're back. How's California?"

"It's good, Uncle Rex." I give him all the smile I can muster.

As she passes me, my aunt squeezes my shoulder in thanks for not making a scene. I only do it for her. I've always hated the way everyone pretends nothing is wrong and refuses to call my uncle out on his shit. The fact that he doesn't even feel the need to explain why he's hours late shows nothing has changed in my absence.

I'm quiet for the rest of dinner, stewing over the kind of

men my uncle and father are. Lee would never do this. He would have been helping me make dinner. Or maybe even prepare it and let me sleep in.

As if a bolt of lightning comes down, the truth hits me. I could never rely on my dad or my uncle growing up, but since he's come back into my life, Lee has worked to prove to me that I'm number one in his life. He saved me the night of the gala, during my plumbing problems, and took the chance of missing another game to take care of me when I was sick.

He's a better man than either of the two men at this table.

Suddenly I feel foolish for pushing him away. I still don't know how we'll handle the work situation, but we'll figure it out together.

And I can't wait to tell him as soon as I get back to San Francisco tomorrow.

———

The plane lands, and all I want to do is call Lee and tell him how wrong I was and how sorry I am for our fight before I left for my parents'. I don't know what we're going to do, but I believe him now when he says we'll figure it out. We just need to come up with a plan.

I usually hate when people stand and wait in the aisle as soon as the plane lands, but today I'm one of them because I'm anxious to see Lee. I don't want to have this conversation over the phone. I want him to be able to look in my eyes and see how much I care for him.

Since I was in and out of Wisconsin, I only have a carry-on with me, so as soon as I'm off the plane, I turn my phone off airplane mode to order an Uber to take me to Lee's place.

It blows up with notifications, all of which I ignore until I order the Uber and see that it's just around the corner. I use the couple of minutes I have to check my texts. First, I text my mom that I landed, then I pull up my thread with Bryce because there are, like, twelve notifications beside her name.

My stomach sinks when I see the picture she texted.

Holy shit.

I'm not sure how long I'm standing there before the Uber pulls up in front of me. I stand in shock, not moving. Finally, the front window rolls down.

"You Shayna? You order an Uber?" the man asks.

I nod, unable to look away from my screen. Then I click on the other text message and swallow against the dryness of my throat. "I need to change the address I'm going to though. That okay?"

He shrugs. "You're the one paying."

My shaking hands can barely open up the door. I slide into the back seat, afraid of what comes next.

thirty-five

. . .

Lee

I step into the Kingsmen owner's office and look at the long faces. Giles is there, of course—it's his office—as well as Coach and Dr. Carlisle.

"Why's everyone look so glum? Bad Thanksgiving with the families?" I ask.

No one responds to my question. Instead, Giles holds out his hand toward one of the chairs across from his desk. "Have a seat, Lee."

I glance at Coach, and he blows out a breath. Dr. Carlisle stands next to him, rigid and asshole-like as usual.

"Someone gonna tell me why I'm here?" I look around the room.

The door to the office opens behind me and I swing around to see who else is joining us. Shayna must've come straight from the airport, because her carry-on suitcase is trailing behind her.

Suddenly, a sinking feeling about what this might be about comes over me. But there's no way they could know anything. We've been careful, despite what Miles thinks. Even if they speculate, there's no proof.

"Thanks for joining us, Ms. Kudrow," Giles says. "Have a seat."

She sits beside me and doesn't look in my direction. "I got here as soon as I could. I just landed."

I shift in my seat, annoyed that they haven't said shit yet. "What's going on?"

Giles opens the drawer to his right and pulls out a manilla envelope. He then removes the contents of the envelope and sets them in front of Shayna and me.

I lean in, spreading the photographs around so I can see them all. They're pictures of me leaving Shayna's building. There aren't any of us together because we've always been careful to never arrive at the same time, but obviously someone has been keeping tabs on me for a while because I'm wearing different outfits.

I push them back toward Giles. "Yeah, so?"

"We know this is Shayna's building."

It's not hard to figure out. The address and street name are beside the entrance to the building, and it's visible in a few of the pictures.

When I glance at Shayna, her face is drained of color and her mouth hangs ajar. She didn't want to come clean, but what choice do we have now?

"Okay fine." I hold up my hands. "I was going to come to you about this sooner, but we had some things to discuss first."

Shayna's head whips in my direction.

"I knew Shayna back in college, and through the process of spending time together since she started working for the Kingsmen, feelings have developed and we're in a relationship."

"Goddammit, Burrows," Coach says, crossing his arms.

Dr. Carlisle frowns and shakes his head like some disapproving father.

Giles stares between us, then opens the drawer to his right

again and pulls out another envelope. "The *San Jose Chronicle* was going to run these pictures, as well as a story about how the Kingsmen quarterback has been having a secret affair with a woman on staff. I had to pay a large sum of money to make the story go away."

I look at Shayna. Bryce has to be the one who ratted us out, which means Shayna's trust was broken. It has to hurt that much more for her.

"I'm sorry, Mr. Hanover, I—" Shayna starts, but he raises his hand to stop her. She presses her lips together.

"As I'm sure you're both aware, we have a no-fraternization policy in the organization. You've both signed papers regarding this policy." He slides some papers out of the envelope and pushes them in Shayna's direction. "Which is why we're relieving you of your duties, Ms. Kudrow, immediately. There's a check enclosed that you'll find will set you up nicely for your next endeavor. You can cash it as soon as you've signed the contract included that states that you entered into a relationship with Mr. Lee Burrows of your own free will and that you were not coerced in any way by him."

I grip the arms of the chair and bolt upright. "What the fuck?"

"Sit down, Lee." Giles's patience is waning with me, but I don't give a shit. He turns his attention back to Shayna. "You'll see we've been more than generous. Feel free to have your lawyer look it over, but you only have twenty-four hours."

With tears in her eyes, Shayna nods and reaches for the papers.

I slap my hand down on them. "She's not signing anything."

"Lee." Her voice is quiet, but it slices me open. She removes my hand, plucking one finger at a time, and takes the papers. She stands. "I'm sorry for any trouble I caused." She turns and takes her carry-on and leaves the room.

"This is bullshit," I say to all three men.

It isn't until I hear the door close behind me that Giles speaks. His fist pounds on the desk. "No, Lee, you listen to me! She's a distraction for you. We can't have you pining over some girl on the sidelines or getting jealous when she's massaging some other player. It never works. There's a reason we have a no-fraternization policy in our contracts."

I stare incredulously at Giles then Coach, who studies the floor. Dr. Carlisle looks smug as though he figured this out weeks ago.

"How come I'm not being punished then?" I ask.

Giles chuckles. "You're not that naive, are you? You're the star. We need your head in the game. We're not going to fire you and ruin your career because you got caught up with a piece of ass. You aren't the first and you won't be the last."

Dr. Carlisle laughs, and I swear to God I've never wanted to punch someone in the face more than I do these two right now.

"That's bullshit and you know it."

"This is the real world, Lee. If you were so concerned for her well-being, you should've thought of that before you fucked her. At any rate, once she signs that contract, the two of you can do whatever you want. It's no longer the organization's problem. But we have to mitigate our losses. We can't be dealing with any Me Too bullshit if things go south with you two."

I push a hand through my hair. "This isn't over." I rush out of the room, anger propelling me forward.

Shayna isn't in the building, nor is she in the parking lot. I need to find her. She's gotta be so upset. This is exactly what she was afraid of, and I blindly thought they'd change the rules for us. Give us a slap on the wrist. Just like Giles said, I was fucking naive.

All I care about right now is holding her, telling her we'll get through this.

thirty-six

. . .

Shayna

The knock at my apartment door doesn't surprise me. I was expecting it after I tucked tail and left Mr. Hanover's office. I don't bother wiping the tears from my face before I swing open my apartment door.

Lee walks right in and wraps me in his arms, and for a brief moment, I allow myself to feel safe. But then everything rushes back to me and I push him away.

"Why did you do that?" I angrily wipe the tears from my cheeks now.

He looks confused for a beat, then his forehead wrinkles. "I didn't leak those pictures."

I roll my eyes.

On the way to the facility from the airport, I read Bryce's frantic texts explaining that someone had tipped off the woman who does the society/gossip portion of the *Chronicle*. I have no idea who tipped off the reporter, but it really doesn't matter at this point. Probably just some random person who wanted to make a quick buck.

"I know you didn't. But why did you admit to everything?"

He throws up his hands. "What was I supposed to say? We were obviously caught."

"Did you stop to think for one second what I might have wanted you to say? You could have come up with a million different excuses—you know someone else in the building, you were picking up something from me to help with your recovery. I don't know. Anything but I've known her since college and we've been sleeping together!" My voice grows louder and louder.

"Well, I'm sorry I didn't think of any of those things. They wouldn't have believed them anyway. They wouldn't have presented us the pictures and brought us in if they weren't sure."

"Maybe not, but they still wouldn't have had proof that we were in a relationship and I wouldn't have gotten fired!" I poke him in the chest, letting my frustration and anger boil over.

"You can't let them fire you."

I almost want to laugh—as though I have a choice. My name isn't Lee Burrows.

"It's already done. You made sure of that." I turn away from him. I can't even look at him.

"I'll talk to my lawyer. There's got to be a loophole or something."

A caustic laugh leaves my lips. "Were you in the same meeting I was? I'm nothing more than a problem to be solved. Sign on the dotted line and fade away, don't cause any trouble for the organization or you."

"So that's it, eh? You're not even going to bother trying to fight for us? To fight for the position you earned?"

I scowl. "You live in la-la land. I'm trying to save what little pride I have left." Crossing my arms, I turn away again.

He steps up behind me and rests his hands on my shoulders. "Look, I understand that you're upset, but we'll figure it out."

I pry myself from his hold and turn to face him. "You keep saying that, but there's nothing to figure out. I lost my job, I'm mortified, and I don't want to go anywhere near the team…"

"Why do I feel like you're talking about me too?"

I swallow past the painful lump in my throat.

He pushes a hand through his hair and steps back. "Jesus, you're just going to walk away from us?"

I shake my head. "I told you this would happen. They're not going to get rid of the star player when they can just as easily buy me off. It was never even a decision for them, Lee. I can't believe you're that jaded."

Guilt covers his features as he comes toward me, but I put out my hand.

"I'm sorry, Shayna. You'll never know how much. But we can get past this." I step farther back when he reaches for me. Fear lights up in his eyes. "What does this mean for us?"

"I don't know. I really don't. But I need you to leave right now. I have to be alone." I wrap my arms around myself and look away from him.

"I'm sorry, shy pie."

I squeeze my eyes shut against the sting of tears at the use of my nickname. "I'll reach out when I know what it means for us."

I can't bear to watch as he silently leaves my apartment. We might never come back from this.

———

It's Sunday, and Bryce came over to spend the day with me so that I'm not tempted to turn the game on just for a glimpse of Lee. The Kingsmen are playing New Orleans today, and all morning, all I've been able to think about is what I *would* be doing today if I was still working for the Kingsmen.

Prepping and taping players, going over any new injuries with the medical staff. Not moping on my couch with a

Tupperware bin of Christmas cookies my mom sent home with me and a full pitcher of sangria.

"Do you want to watch *Bachelor in Paradise* next or binge-watch *Bridgerton* again?" Bryce asks with my remote in her hands.

"There's probably more heartbreak on *Bachelor in Paradise,* so let's watch that."

With a nod, she speaks it into the remote. "Did you reach out to a lawyer to go over the Kingsmen's offer yet?"

Her voice is hesitant and for good reason. I haven't wanted to discuss the contract they handed me on Friday—it was like pouring salt into an infected wound.

I shake my head and refill my glass with sangria. "I'm not taking their offer."

"Good for you. Squeeze those assholes for every dime they're worth." She presses the button once the show comes up in the search.

"No, you misunderstand me. I'm not taking any money from them. It's insulting that they think they need to pay me off to keep me from causing problems. I'm an adult. I went into the relationship with Lee with my eyes wide open. I won't give them the satisfaction of signing that contract and cashing that check like I was a whore who seduced him."

Bryce gives me what I think is a proud smile. "I take back what I said earlier about squeezing them for every penny. Your plan is much better."

"Thanks. And thanks for coming over today to keep me from wallowing."

She chuckles. "Well, you're definitely still wallowing, but that's to be expected. Your life just imploded."

I give her a wan smile, pulling the blanket over my legs. "Thanks."

She stares at me for a beat, then opens her mouth to say something but closes it.

"What?"

She shakes her head. "Nothing." She sips her sangria.

"You were going to say something."

"I was, but I forget now." She waves me off.

I tilt my chin down and look at her from under my eyebrows. "You're not one to school your thoughts. Speak."

She sighs. "Fine. I was going to ask if you've reached out to Lee, but I didn't know if you'd want to talk about it if you did." She cringes.

"He's texted a few times, but I ignored him." In truth, I blocked his number. "I'm not ready to talk to him. I'm still angry at him. I feel like the first chance he had to go with his plan, he jumped at the opportunity without thinking about how it might affect me. And honestly, I'm pissed at myself for getting into this situation in the first place. It's going to take me time to untangle my feelings over being fired and losing everything I've worked for, and to separate that from my anger at Lee specifically and just my anger in general. My head is a mess."

I let my head flop back against the couch and stare at the ceiling. Bryce squeezes my hand, and I lift my head and look at her.

"I'm here for you no matter what you decide."

"Thanks. One thing is for sure, no matter what comes of this mess my life is in right now, I'm glad I took the job, otherwise I never would have met you."

We both have tears in our eyes as we hug it out. At least something good came of this mess.

thirty-seven

· · ·

Lee

"Cheer up, buttercup. I'm sure she'll come around." Brady clinks his beer against mine.

"It's been two weeks and she still has me blocked. Still won't answer the door when I go by." I bring the beer to my lips.

We're hanging out at Brady's because he has his son tonight, but it's after Theo's bedtime, so he's upstairs sleeping.

Being here reminds me of the night of the Halloween party and how fucking hot Shayna looked. Our make-out session in the guest room and how I convinced her to go home with me.

"Man up and move on." Chase shakes his head. "Do you have any idea how much pussy there is out there for you? Hell, you're Lee fucking Burrows!"

It's the most I've heard Chase say in a long time.

"Don't you think I would if I could?" I scowl at him on the other sofa. "I don't want anybody else, just her."

Miles looks between the three of us as though he wants to add in his two cents, but he stays uncharacteristically quiet when it comes to my life.

These three guys are the only ones who know everything that went down. I trust them, and they've been good friends to me since Shayna stopped speaking to me. Still, it doesn't make it any easier to ignore the giant crater in my chest when I think of her—which is, like, every other second.

"She really did a number on you." Chase takes a pull of his beer.

I scowl at him. "I can't wait until you fall for someone someday and see what torture this is. I'm gonna laugh my ass off."

That comment gets a rare smile out of him. "Never gonna happen."

"Never say never," Miles says.

"You guys, our friend has suffered a deep emotional trauma. It's not to be made light of," Brady says in a serious voice, then laughs.

I pick up the small football on the end table and throw it at Brady, but the fucker catches it of course.

He holds up his hands. "I should insure these things." He shrugs his shoulder and drinks his beer.

This is what I mean by them being good friends. Sometimes they're there to listen to me complain and whine, and other times they bust my balls to make me laugh.

"So what are you going to do? Seriously?" Brady asks, leaning back into the couch and propping his beer on his thigh.

I shake my head. "I don't know. Sometimes I think the best approach is to leave her alone and let her come to me when she's ready, but then other times I think, 'Fight, motherfucker, you're not some loser who stands by and watches what you want slip out of your hands.'"

"Women are complicated," Brady says. "Listen to this. I had this one-night stand and she was fucking amazing in bed. Like, probably the best I've had, maybe ever."

"Ever?" Chase asks with raised eyebrows.

"I'm telling you, I beat off like twice a day still and it was weeks ago. Anyway, afterward, I ask for her number." He points at himself. "*I'm* asking for *her* number. I don't want to sound conceited, but I'm Brady Banks, Kingsmen wide receiver. Guess what she says?"

We all wait, although I bet I already know. I'm surprised he's even telling us this, because we'll be able to razz him forever.

"'No, thanks.'" His face is straight, no emotion except disbelief. "She said no thanks."

Chase laughs, like a full-on belly laugh, which spurs Miles and me to do the same.

"Fuck, guys, it's not funny. I swear she was a gymnast or some shit, because I can't stop beating off every time one glimpse of that night resurfaces."

Chase continues to laugh. Brady throws the football at him, which he catches because we're all awesome like that.

The room quiets and I'm back to thinking about Shayna again.

"What you need is a grand gesture."

We all turn to look at Miles with different versions of confused faces.

"What the fuck is a grand gesture?" Chase asks.

"It's where you do something really big and momentous after you fuck up." Miles sets his beer on the table beside the beanbag he's sitting in that's obviously Brady's son's.

"Sure, send her, like, two dozen red roses," Chase says.

Miles rolls his eyes and shakes his head. "First of all, I'm impressed you could even think that romantically." Chase throws the football at Miles, and he tucks it under his arm. "But I said really big and momentous. Think something more like… renting out The Palace ballroom and sending her an invitation to an event, but when she gets there, it's only you waiting for her."

"With red roses," Chase says, and Brady cracks up.

Miles glares at Chase. "Or hire a skywriter to write I'm sorry in the sky, or even something like whisking her away on a surprise tropical vacation but giving her none of the details beforehand."

"She won't talk to him. How would he get her to go on vacation with him?" Chase asks.

"I hate to be a buzzkill, but he's got a point." Brady cringes.

The football flies across the room at Chase, and he's too busy laughing with Brady. He misses it and an assembled Lego set crashes to the hardwood.

"Fuck!" Brady puts down his beer and runs over behind the couch. "Theo is going to have a meltdown. It took us weeks to finish this."

"You sound scared of your own kid?" Chase says.

"You would be too, if you saw his reaction to this."

Chase rounds the couch and picks up the pieces with Brady. "Give me a half hour."

Once we're all back together, Brady brings in another round of beers. Chase is somehow putting together the Lego set without directions or a picture.

"Let's get back to Miles being a closet romantic," Brady says, laughing.

"Whatever, asshole. I heard my mom and my sister talking about it when they came to visit, so I asked them what it meant. Apparently it's in all the romance books they read. Women eat that kinda stuff up."

"Grand gesture." I set down my beer and pace Brady's large living room, hands on my hips. "What kind of grand gesture would fit us?"

Nobody says anything for a minute until Chase offers up his idea. "Maybe you get her box seats for one of the games and have something on the jumbotron."

Miles shakes his head. "She's not gonna want to hang out and watch a game of the team that just fired her."

Chase shrugs and shows emotion when he finds the piece to go in a specific spot. Who knew we just needed to get Chase a Legos set for him to show some emotion?

"Thanks for the suggestion though," I tell Chase. Then I look between all three of them. "Okay, what other ideas have you guys got?"

"You could fly her family in and profess your love for her in front of them," Brady says.

I shake my head. "She's not that close to her dad and I've never met them. I'd really like the first time I do to not be when I'm begging for forgiveness."

Brady scratches his head. "Good point."

"What does she want more than anything?" Miles asks. "Maybe you could get her that."

I ponder his question for a minute, thinking back to whether I ever heard her mention a purse or designer shoes or a car she'd want. But then I think of his question in a different way.

What she really wanted was to be able to keep her job and for us to be together out in the open.

An idea hits me like the punch of a heavyweight boxer.

"I know what I have to do." I walk back across the room and pick up my phone off the table, scrolling through my contacts until I find Jaron's.

With a deep breath, I hit his name and leave the room so that he and I can have a private conversation. He's not going to be happy. But I don't care.

I meant it when I said I'd do anything for the woman I love.

thirty-eight

. . .

Shayna

It's been a little less than three weeks since I've seen or talked to Lee. It's getting harder and harder not to unblock his number and call him. During a moment of weakness the other night, I Google searched him. I just needed to see his face.

Now that a lot of my anger has passed, I can see that he didn't intentionally hurt me or use the situation to get what he wanted, but it doesn't make it any easier to swallow that I'm the one who ended up paying the price while he was unaffected by our relationship. Still, I owe him a conversation at the very least.

I'm meeting Bryce at her place, then we're going to head out to do some Christmas shopping. I'll be leaving for home in about a week and will stay with my parents over the holidays. When I return, it's time to start looking for a new job.

It won't be my dream job with a professional football team, because I can't tell them about my experience and have them get a reference that I screwed the quarterback, but it could be worse.

Once I've parked and backtracked the couple blocks to Bryce's building, my phone goes off in my purse. I pull it out in case Bryce is telling me she's running late, but it's a notification from the sports app. I click on it as I'm walking through the lobby door to Bryce's building and gasp when I read the headline.

Rumors Spread That Kingsmen Quarterback Wants Out of San Francisco

I read the article as fast as possible. It states Lee is apparently going to be a free agent after the year is up and is looking at either Los Angeles or Seattle. He has no interest in staying with the team when he said only months ago San Francisco was his home.

"What the hell?" I whisper. A door opens and I slide over to allow the person to pass.

"I'm assuming you just saw the article?"

Bryce's voice pulls my attention away from my phone. She's standing in the doorway looking as chic as always.

"Why would he want to leave the Kingsmen? It makes no sense. He wanted to stay in San Francisco."

"Dunno. But man am I pissed they got the scoop before I did. My boss is going to have my ass tomorrow."

"I was just thinking that I was going to call him later so we could talk, but I guess it doesn't matter now if he's moving. Is he moving to get away from me?"

"Hey." Bryce grips my upper arm. "You've run him out of town because everything he sees reminds him of you."

A sad smile forms on my lips. "I don't know what this is. I mean, he fought so hard to get us back together and I made a rash decision, but would he really just move away?"

She rubs my arm, giving me a compassionate look. "Do you still want to go shopping or do you want to do it a different time?"

I shake my head. "No, I have to get something for my parents before I fly home." I suck in a deep breath through my nose. "I'll reach out to him later, but I can't wallow every time I see Lee's name in the news. It's not healthy."

"If you're sure…"

I nod. "I am."

She hooks her arm through mine and leads the way out of the building. "All right. I know this cute little shop a couple of blocks up that sells the most adorable handmade bags. Maybe they're something your mom might like."

"Lead the way."

It's impossible not to think of Lee all afternoon as I pass kids and adults with his jersey on, but I force myself not to wallow. At least now that I've made the decision to talk to him, I don't feel as much like I'm in limbo. By the end of the day, I should have some certainty or closure on what I had with Lee.

———

I arrive home right before dinner, and when I step off the elevator onto my floor, I come to a stop. Lee's sitting on the floor with his back against my door.

He stands as soon as he sees me. "Hey, sorry. I needed to talk to you and figured this would be the best way to catch you since you're avoiding me."

My cheeks heat because we both know I blocked him.

I walk toward my door, pulling my key from my purse. "I was actually going to call you tonight."

He looks at the floor and pushes a hand through his hair. "You heard the news. That's why I'm here."

I unlock the door and push it open, leaving it ajar for Lee to follow me inside. "I did, yeah. Have to say… I'm surprised."

"The goddamn press… always breaking news before I'm

ready." He closes the door behind him then looks around my living room as though he's trying to catalog it for changes.

It's weird to have him back in my space again, but not in a bad way. In a way, it makes me realize how barren and empty the place has felt since he was last here. I hang my purse and my coat on the hook near my front door, then turn to face him.

"What are you talking about?"

He throws up his hands. "I had a whole grand gesture I was working on, and those assholes screwed it up with that report."

A smile ticks up one corner of my lips. "Grand gesture?"

"Yeah, you must know what that is, right? You're a girl. I assume you do. Miles said something about romance novels?"

I cross my arms and press my lips together to keep from laughing. He seems so thoroughly miffed, it's hard not to find him funny. "I understand the general concept, yes."

"It doesn't matter now."

"Why don't you give me the general gist of what is involved?"

He follows me to sit on the couch. "I was brainstorming grand gesture ideas with the guys—"

I hold up my hand. "Wait. You and the guys were sitting around talking about ways you could win me back?"

He nods and gives me a look like "of course we were." "Yeah. Miles asked me what you want most and I knew the answer was to have your job at the Kingsmen back and for us to be together." He looks at me with question-filled eyes—did he get it right?

I debate playing harder to get, but the truth is, I've missed this man. Any ire I felt at losing my job is now appropriately directed at Giles Hanover, so I nod.

He blows out a relieved breath. "So I called Jaron and told

him to start working on getting me traded to Seattle or Los Angeles when my contract is up."

"I don't understand. Why?"

He takes my hands. "It's not fair that you're the only one who lost something. I was naive not to figure they'd do exactly what you told me they would do. And you tried to warn me, but I thought I knew better. I realize now that because I've been in a position of privilege for so long, I got used to things working out for me. So I told Jaron, Seattle or Los Angeles because they're the closest for me to fly back and forth to San Francisco, where you are. If I leave, you're free to get your job back—if that's something you want—and even if you don't, it just seemed right that I should make a sacrifice too."

I'm speechless for a moment as I replay everything he said over again in my head. My hands come up to cover my mouth. "You left the Kingsmen for me?"

He looks so hopeful when he nods.

"You stupid man." I stand. "There's no sense in both of us losing what we want."

He looks stunned for a beat. "I thought this would make you happy. It's my grand gesture."

I bring my palm to his face. "Watching you lose your dream does not make me happy. Besides, I wouldn't go back to work for that asshole Giles Hanover anyway. I'll figure something else out."

"Shayna, I can replace my job, but I can't replace you."

Tears well in my eyes and I sniff to keep them from falling. "I don't want you to leave the Kingsmen. Not unless that's what you want. I know Seattle and Los Angeles aren't that far, but if we're going to be able to openly be in a relationship, I want to be able to see you all the time."

He smiles, and his eyes light up from the inside. Then he brings his hands to my cheeks and our lips meet.

His taste, his scent, his feel, it all comes rushing back to me. I wrap my arms around him, deepening the kiss.

He pulls away and looks me straight in the eyes. "I love you, shy pie. From now on, we make decisions about the big stuff together. Deal?"

I nod, biting my bottom lip. "Deal."

Lee kisses me again. Before long, our clothes are being pulled off and tossed all over the room.

"Wait." I place my hand on his chest from where I straddle him, right before he unhooks my bra.

"I feel like I've been waiting forever." He's practically panting, and I can't help but laugh.

"Would you like to come with me to Wisconsin over Christmas to meet my parents? I know you don't have a lot of days off, but even a quick visit… I really want them to meet you."

He grins and pulls me in for a hard kiss.

"You couldn't keep me away." He unhooks my bra and my breasts fall out.

"I did and look how well that turned out."

"Sometimes we learn from failure."

"Yes, we do." I moan as he pulls my nipple into his mouth and we lose ourselves in each other's bodies.

I'm exactly where I'm supposed to be, bumps in the roads and all. We each have one another's backs as we walk into the future.

epilogue

. . .

Lee

Six Months Later…

As we settle in the large SUV and the driver hoists our suitcases into the back, I kiss Shayna. Her skin is sun kissed from our two weeks sailing around the Mediterranean with my brother and his wife.

I remembered the way Shayna stared longingly at the superyacht cruise at the silent auction during the Kingsmen gala last year, so when we talked about what we might want to do during the off-season, I knew this had to be it. The hard part was convincing her to take two weeks off work. She's working at a high-end therapy clinic—something that still fills me with guilt—but she insists she's happy. I believe her, but I know she'd rather be working at her old job with the Kingsmen.

It seems unfair that I'm still living my dream and she doesn't get to, but she's insistent that there's no point in me giving up my dream—it won't make either of us feel any better. I suppose she's right, but that doesn't mean I don't feel like an ass.

Hence why I wanted to spoil her with a private yacht

vacation. And the fact that she was able to get to know my brother and his wife and vice versa was an added bonus. She and Jana are thick as thieves now—something that I think might come to bite Kane and me in the ass down the road.

"I don't think I've ever felt so relaxed." She leans back into the leather seat with a smile. "Or well fed. I swear they have the best food in Europe."

"Tell me about it." I rub my stomach. "I'm going to have to work out twice a day to get ready for training camp."

The driver climbs in, clicks on his seat belt, and puts the SUV in drive to pull away from the curb.

Shayna grins and whispers in my ear, "You know, I'm a trained professional and I can think of a few ways to burn off some calories when we get home."

My dick jumps and I suppress a groan. "I can't wait for you to show me them."

Her phone dings in her purse and she draws back to dig it out. "Oh, it's Bryce wanting to know all about our trip."

She starts texting, and I realize I haven't even turned my phone back on since we got off the plane. I pull it from my pocket and slide the power button on, waiting for it to connect. A bunch of notifications go off, most of which I ignore. There are some text messages, so I go there first.

One is from Kane, making sure we arrived home safely, another from Miles, and there's one from a number I don't recognize. I click on it to read the message.

Hi Lee. I hope you don't mind me reaching out. This is Jasper Banks, Brady's father. I'm looking to get in touch with Shayna, but Brady didn't have her number so I'm texting you. I heard you're arriving home today, and I had hoped to meet with her ASAP upon her return. Is this something you can facilitate?

. . .

My forehead wrinkles.

"Everything okay?" Shayna asks. I hand her my phone so she can read the message, then she's looking at me with drawn eyebrows. "Why would Brady's dad want to meet with me?"

I shrug. "No clue."

"Well, what do you know about him?"

I think back to what Brady may have mentioned. It's not like I've researched my buddy's dad. "I know he's megarich. Got his start in venture capital, I think. Brady's stepmom has money too. She owns some sex toy company."

Shayna chuckles. "Seriously? Which one?"

I shrug again. "I don't know. From what Brady says, she's quite something though."

She bites her lip. "I guess text him back and see when he wants to meet. That's the only way to know what's going on."

After a few texts back and forth with Jasper, I give the driver Jasper's address and ask him if he'd mind waiting while we take a quick meeting.

"It's on your dime." He looks at me in the rearview mirror, not seeming to care a whole lot.

Jasper lives in Pacific Heights, only a few blocks away from Brady. It's a massive mansion that screams money and looks to be four stories. I bet it has killer views of the bay on the backside.

"Wow. And I thought Brady's house was nice," Shayna whispers when we pull up, as though the people inside the house can hear us.

"Do you want me to come in with you?" I ask Shayna when her hand goes to the door handle.

She looks at me over her shoulder with wide eyes. "Absolutely! I'm not going in there by myself."

I chuckle. "All right. Just wanted to check."

I tell the driver we'll be back as soon as we can, and we make our way up the steps to the large, arched double doors. They open before I even have a chance to ring the bell. The woman at the door has shoulder-length dark hair and full sleeves of tattoos peeking out of her T-shirt.

"Hi, I'm Lee Burrows and this is Shayna Kudrow. We're here to meet with Mr. Banks."

She smiles wide and opens the door wider in invitation. "Don't let Jasper hear you call him that. He insists it ages him to old man status."

I chuckle and we follow her inside.

She puts out her hand. "I'm Lennon, Jasper's wife."

With a house this big, I'm surprised they don't have a butler.

"You have a beautiful home," Shayna says, looking around.

"Thank you. Jasper told me to keep an eye out for you. He's just in his office, working." She rolls her eyes. "Always working, that one. More than me. Anyway, I'll take you to him."

She leads us toward the back of the home, and every hallway contains framed pictures of a younger Brady and two other kids who I think are twins. We go up two levels and walk down a hallway until we reach a closed door. I think I might get lost if I lived here.

Lennon knocks softly on the door, then opens it. "Babe. Your guests are here." She looks at us. "Good luck. Hope I'll be seeing a lot more of you." She winks and walks away.

Shayna looks at me, probably wondering, as I am, what she meant by that comment.

"C'mon in, you two."

We look inside the office. Sitting behind a large desk is a man I suspect Brady will look a lot like in twenty or so years. He has some gray at the temples, but he's fit for his age and is dressed in slacks and a polo shirt.

He stands and comes around the desk with his hand out.

"Jasper Banks, good to meet you both. Brady has nothing but nice things to say about you both."

We each shake his hand, then he leads us to a sitting area with a couch and two chairs. Shayna and I sit side by side on the couch and he takes one of the chairs.

"I'm sure you're wondering why I wanted to meet with you." He directs his attention to Shayna.

She shifts in her seat. "Um… a little, yes."

Jasper smiles and it reminds me a lot of Brady. "There will be an announcement tomorrow that my wife and I have purchased the San Francisco Kingsmen football team."

I'm not sure which of us draws in a deep breath first.

"Oh wow, congratulations," she says.

He nods, nonplussed as though it's every day that he purchases a professional football team. "I understand you used to work for the Kingsmen as an athletic trainer."

She nods. "Yes, I was let go about six months ago."

Jasper's lips thin. "Brady filled me in on all that unpleasantness. You should've seen my wife's reaction when she heard. I thought she might jump over the table and strangle old man Hanover." He chuckles as if picturing it, then looks at us. "Part of a purchase this large is due diligence and finding out anything that might be a liability and come back around to bite you in the ass down the road."

Shayna stiffens. "I assure you that I didn't refuse their payoff so that I could come back later and try to sue them."

He waves her off. "Oh, I know that. My son tells me you're good people. I'm not here to mitigate damages. You're here because, from everything I've been told, you're an excellent trainer, and I want to offer you your old position back."

Her mouth drops open. I can't help the smile that transforms my face.

"You should know that Dr. Carlisle's contract will be paid out and he'll no longer be with the organization. We only like people on our team who are positive and look forward. He's just not going to work with the culture we want to build at the Kingsmen."

Thank God. I hate that asshole. I swear he was pissed when I signed my three-year contract with the team at the end of the last season. I'm pretty sure he's the one who had us investigated in the first place.

"I… I don't know what to say."

I take her hand and squeeze it. "Say yes. This is what you want."

She looks between Jasper and me for a moment. "But the two of us… working together…"

Jasper laughs. "Not a problem. It's an existing relationship that we've known about, but you both will have to sign some paperwork that you're both in a committed relationship."

Shayna looks at me, and I nod.

"Yes, I accept. Thank you so much." Her eyes overfill with happiness, reminding me of the glittering sea we just left behind.

"Wonderful. Happy to have you as part of the team. And Lee…" He turns to face me. "I can't wait to see what you and Brady pull off on the field this season."

"Me too, sir."

He opens his mouth, but the office door bursts open before he gets a word out.

"Dad, I have a problem." Brady stands in the doorway, his hair disheveled and his clothes wrinkly. Not at all like he usually looks. "Oh shit, sorry. I didn't know you were in a meeting. Hey guys." He raises his hand in hello and we follow suit. "Looks like I managed the grand gesture, Burrows. Getting your girl her job back and all." Brady winks.

I shake my head but let that go for now, since we're in his parents' house and his dad is going to be my new boss.

"Go ahead, Lee, kick his ass," Jasper says. I already know I'm going to enjoy working for this man.

"I'll be in the kitchen." Brady goes to shut the door.

Jasper stands. "Everything okay, Brady?"

Brady looks between his dad, Shayna, and me before blowing out a breath. "You guys might as well hear it too." He steps in and shuts the door. "The new nanny Hannah hired? It's the woman from that one-night stand who wouldn't give me her number."

"The gymnast?" I ask.

He laughs but bites his inner cheek. "Can you fucking believe it?"

"No," I say.

"Me either. It's like a romance novel." Brady shakes his head.

"What am I missing?" Shayna asks.

I look at Brady. "You can't kiss the nanny, Brady Banks."

"And that's the problem." He points at me.

He's screwed, and after what Shayna and I went through to be together, I can't wait to watch one of my friends squirm.

The End

cockamamie unicorn ramblings

Well, what did you think of your first foray into the Kingsmen football team?

When it came time to wrap up the Hockey Hotties series, we weren't sure whether to continue with hockey or venture into a new sport. We remembered the very unscientific poll in our Facebook reader group before we started writing Hockey Hotties, asking what sport readers love the most. Football and hockey came out almost even. So, we decided to switch things up knowing that if readers weren't digging the football we could jump into hockey again.

BUT, we hope we've convinced you to stick around for the rest of our football romances because we've outlined the next few books and they're going to be a lot of fun!

When we originally talked about this book, we wanted to do an enemies-to-lovers trope (one of our favorites) and a second chance romance. Proximity is always tricky with sports romance because the truth is the average heroine doesn't get in close contact with professional athletes (other-wise we'd all be chasing NHL and NFL players right!? LOL) So we added workplace romance to the mix!

Once that was settled, we needed to ask the question, "WHY does Shayna hate Brady at the beginning of the book". We settled on a bet... something we don't think we've done before, but if we have we're sure you'll let us know. If you haven't already read False Start, the free prequel to the KIngsmen Football Stars series and you want to see exactly how it all went down you can go back and read, it's free!

Writing the first book in a series is always hard—there's so many new characters and you have to figure out their individual personalities, what they stand for and be mindful of what you write because eventually you'll have to live up to it when you get to their book. Believe us when we say that we've written some things in the past we wish we could take back because it made it so hard when it came time to write that specific character's book.

But we're totally invested in all our characters and hope you are too. We've got some fun things planned for them in the future. Just wait and see!

There's always so many people to thank who help with our books…

The entire Valentine PR Team.
Cassie from Joy Editing for line edits.
Ellie from My Brother's Editor for line edits.
Rosa from My Brother's Editor for proofreading.
Hang Le for the cover and branding for the entire series.
Bloggers who read, review and/or promote our work. Thank you for helping to spread the word!
All the Piper Rayne Unicorns who are so supportive and positive about our work! Thank you seems too little to say but know we are grateful beyond measure.

Every reader who took the time to read our story—whether it's your first Piper Rayne book or your fiftieth. We hope we provided you with a few hours of entertainment, some laughs and a boost in the libido.

Now, we're onto Brady Banks. You might remember him as that cute little boy from Mad About the Banker. Well, he's all grown up now with a son of his own. And he's found himself in an impossible predicament, wanting to kiss the nanny. Stay tuned!

Xo,
Piper & Rayne

about piper & rayne

Piper Rayne is a USA Today Bestselling Author duo who write "heartwarming humor with a side of sizzle" about families, whether that be blood or found. They both have e-readers full of one-clickable books, they're married to husbands who drive them to drink, and they're both chauffeurs to their kids. Most of all, they love hot heroes and quirky heroines who make them laugh, and they hope you do, too!

also by piper rayne

Kingsmen Football Stars

You had your chance, Lee Burrows

You can't kiss the Nanny, Brady Banks

Over my Brother's Dead Body, Chase Andrews

The Modern Love World

Charmed by the Bartender

Hooked by the Boxer

Mad about the Banker

The Single Dad's Club

Real Deal

Dirty Talker

Sexy Beast

Hollywood Hearts

Mister Mom

Animal Attraction

Domestic Bliss

Bedroom Games

Cold as Ice

On Thin Ice

Break the Ice

Box Set

Charity Case

Manic Monday

Afternoon Delight

Happy Hour

Blue Collar Brothers

Flirting with Fire

Crushing on the Cop

Engaged to the EMT

White Collar Brothers

Sexy Filthy Boss

Dirty Flirty Enemy

Wild Steamy Hook-up

The Rooftop Crew

My Bestie's Ex

A Royal Mistake

The Rival Roomies

Our Star-Crossed Kiss

The Do-Over

A Co-Workers Crush

Hockey Hotties

My Lucky #13

The Trouble with #9

Faking it with #41

Sneaking around with #34

Second Shot with #76

Offside with #55

The Baileys

Lessons from a One-Night Stand

Advice from a Jilted Bride

Birth of a Baby Daddy

Operation Bailey Wedding (Novella)

Falling for My Brother's Best Friend

Demise of a Self-Centered Playboy

Confessions of a Naughty Nanny

Operation Bailey Babies (Novella)

Secrets of the World's Worst Matchmaker

Winning My Best Friend's Girl

Rules for Dating your Ex

Operation Bailey Birthday (Novella)

The Greenes

My Beautiful Neighbor

My Almost Ex

My Vegas Groom

The Greene Family Summer Bash

My Sister's Flirty Friend

My Unexpected Surprise

My Famous Frenemy

The Greene Family Vacation

My Scorned Best Friend

My Fake Fiancé

My Brother's Forbidden Friend

My Greene Family Christmas

Lake Starlight

The Problem with Second Chances